SILENT SONG

Leslie Knowles

ZEBRA BOOKS
KENSINGTON PUBLISHING CORP.

ZEBRA BOOKS are published by

Kensington Publishing Corp.
850 Third Avenue
New York, NY 10022

Copyright © 1996 by Leslie Knowles

All rights reserved. No part of this book may be reproduced in any form or by any means without the prior written consent of the Publisher, excepting brief quotes used in reviews.

If you purchased this book without a cover, you should be aware that this book is stolen property. It was reported as "unsold and destroyed" to the Publisher and neither the Author nor the Publisher has received any payment for this "stripped book."

Zebra and the Z logo Reg. U.S. Pat. & TM Off.

First Printing: June, 1996
10 9 8 7 6 5 4 3 2 1

Printed in the United States of America

One

"Okay, girls, let's try it again. Kristen, watch your support arch. You're letting it roll in during the *rond de jamb*."

Nicole Michaels' voice reached Jake Cameron through the glass observation doors of the ballet studio, and the sharp pain it caused surprised him. After five years he hadn't thought something so simple as her voice could bring it all back so swiftly, and it angered him that it did.

He settled his long frame against the rich wood paneling beside the door so he could watch her work. She still wore her glossy chestnut hair pulled tightly into a coil at the base of her neck, and the thin-strapped, black leotard with the pale pink tights and satin point shoes gave the same fragile impression he remembered. A bitter smile touched his lips and faded. She was about as fragile as a Mack truck. That deceptively delicate frame covered a will of iron.

She demonstrated a graceful arabesque and the line of her arms and legs presented the seemingly effortless perfection that came with years of training and supreme control. The ballet fit her personality. Its discipline gave a gossamer covering for the passion and fire of the dance . . . and underneath her calm, unruffled exterior, Nicole smoldered with passion and fire.

Jake's body tightened, remembering the sensation of touching the soft skin covering those firm muscles and the excitement of making her lose control until she clung to him, breathless and sated. He stifled a curse. He didn't want to remember the good times. All the good times amounted to nothing when he thought of the cold deliberation with which she told him her career was more important than the pregnancy neither of them had planned. She had refused his offer of marriage with no more remorse than her face showed now.

Nicole finished demonstrating the next combination and turned toward the record player beside the door to set it to music. When the shadow in the lobby caught her attention, she looked up. Shock waves washed over her, chilling her skin and making her heart race with fear. *Jake.* Dear God, how had he found her? He must know something. That thought turned her fear into panic. *Brianna's mine—he can't have her!*

He was leaning against the wall the same way he had the first time she'd met him, watching her just as closely as he did now. But then his eyes had been warm with approval; tonight their glacial blue froze her with condemnation. The carefully trimmed beard he'd grown since she left did little to soften the hard line of his mouth. She could see it was set with tightly held anger, and something inside lurched as she remembered how sensuously teasing it could be when he smiled. He didn't smile now, though, and she had to turn away from the grim satisfaction that told her he knew she'd seen him.

Her hand shook as she tried to reset the record player. Whatever feelings he'd had for her had died. She'd killed them with a lie that had torn her apart even though she knew she'd never had a real choice. But time hadn't lessened the intensity of her reaction to him, and she knew she would have to pull herself together. If he wanted Brianna, Nicole would fight him. He might have the money and power of fame, but Brianna belonged with her.

Nicole took a deep breath and put the needle into the groove. Turning back to her class she was relieved to see that the time-stopping moment hadn't been more than seconds, and her class had noticed nothing wrong. At least, not with her. They had noticed Jake, though, and they whispered together excitedly, sending shy glances in his direction. She clapped her hands sharply to regain their attention.

"Starting positions. And . . . one . . . two . . . three . . . four . . . and *pique releve*—that's right."

Determinedly, she took them through the exercise several more times before dismissing the class for the evening. She reminded them they had costume fittings the following week, but doubted if they heard her as they surrounded Jake asking for autographs.

He couldn't ignore their requests, and for once Nicole appreciated his active sense of duty. She needed more time to compose herself before their confrontation. The look he shot her over her students' heads told her it would be no fond reunion.

She watched him sign the odd assortment of notebook paper, scrap envelopes, and store receipts, but shock blocked all coherent thought. She noted that his dark hair was longer, curling into his collar. His gaunt frame had filled out, its lean maturity showing his success. She remembered their poverty days together and doubted if he lived on peanut butter and cheap fast food anymore.

Nicole sorted through the albums, straightening them while he finished signing the last piece of paper. Jake waited until they were alone before turning toward her. She forced herself to leave the ballroom and approach him.

She had forgotten how small he made her feel when he towered over her. Long ago his size had made her feel safe and protected. Now he made her feel vulnerable and defenseless. She fought the urge to run and hide as she had done so long ago. The time had come to meet him without giving ground. Her nerves taut, she took a steadying breath, and faced him squarely. She prayed her voice would remain steady.

"Hello, Jake. It's been a long time."

"It wouldn't have been so long if you had left a forwarding address."

Nicole heard all the irony in his bitter answer, and the guilt she had buried for five years resurfaced, fresh and solid. "How did you find me?"

"I hired an investigator."

"Why?" The word was torn from her, ripping away from her throat with raw fear. She forced the panic down. "After five years, why bother?"

"I had to know what happened to you." His glare was direct and accusing. "When you never showed up as soloist with the company—"

For the first time, Nicole noticed the faint lines etched around Jake's eyes. He had done more than matured. There was something in the deep blue eyes, something beyond the lines, that had not been there when they were lovers. It wasn't pain, though. It couldn't be. A man had to allow himself to care more deeply than Jake did for pain to leave permanent traces. But there was something there. Cynicism? Yes . . . and determination.

Jake was caring, she amended. Despite all the times he'd made it clear he had no plans for marriage, he'd cared enough to feel responsible when she found herself pregnant. But his offer to marry her had been the concern of an honorable man. He hadn't loved her. They were two different things.

"If it mattered that much, why wait five years?" Nicole felt her skin flash first hot then cold at the thought of a private investigator spying on her . . . on Brianna. Jake hadn't mentioned her yet. An investigator would include such an obvious part of her life in his report. Was he waiting for her to break down and confess?

"Look, you walked out on me, remember?" His voice was harsh and taunting.

"You told me to get out."

"You knew I didn't mean it. We were both blowing off steam."

"You meant it. You could have found me long before this if you hadn't."

"No one would tell me where you were. You have very loyal friends." His smile was as humorless as his gaze was cold. "Since you so obviously didn't want to be found, I figured I might as well accept a few tour offers I'd been thinking about. By the time I got back and realized you'd disappeared for good, Adam and David still weren't talking." He ran his fingers through his dark hair, the familiar gesture telling Nicole more than his words how frustrated he was. He looked up, his gaze pinning her with demand. "Why did you leave the company?"

"I left the company because I was pregnant, and you know it," Nicole stated flatly. "Didn't the investigator give you the complete history?"

"I just told him to find out where you were, not to spy." Jake retorted. "I wanted you to be the one to answer my questions, not some stranger who peeked in windows."

"What questions, Jake?" Nicole struggled to remain calm. Maybe he didn't know about Brianna.

"Questions like why you still haunted my dreams and whether you were ever worth all the pain and guilt you left me with," Jake said bitterly. "Hell, I had to know how someone so crazy about kids could refuse to keep it because it might slow down a dancing career—" He broke off, then continued with a quiet taunt. "What happened, Nicole? How did someone as ambitious and talented as you end up teaching in San Bernardino when you could have performed with any company in the world?"

He doesn't know. Nicole absorbed the certainty along with the bitterness and frustration she saw in his eyes. Maybe she'd been wrong. Maybe it *was* pain that left those dark traces in his eyes. Only it wasn't because of her. It was the baby and the threats she'd made. She couldn't lie to him again.

"I think you've always known, Jake. Why else would you still need to find me?"

Jake's skin tightened as a chill lifted the hairs on his arms and the back of his neck. Did that mean—It must. She'd had his baby after all.

But why had she lied to him, then run away? He'd offered to marry her, damn it! He hadn't hesitated to accept his responsibility for getting her pregnant. Hell, he'd even offered to give up his music career and take a job with his father's accounting firm so they'd have a regular paycheck.

She had my baby.

Realization hit, and his skin sent another ripple of shock through his system. The chill was immediately followed by a flash of heat that warmed into euphoria and left him dazed and disoriented.

I'm a father. The words sang through him, echoing through his mind in harmonic chorus. Some part of him asked the question he had to know. "Was it a boy or a girl?" His voice sounded distant to his ears, filtered through the ongoing echo, *father . . . father . . . father. . . .*

"A girl."

He came back with a jolt. Nicole watched him with a half-defiant, half-guilty look. "Did you keep—"

"Yes. I named her Brianna."

Brianna. He had a daughter named Brianna. Jake closed his eyes to let the pain and joy of that knowledge wash over him. When he opened them again, his gaze pierced Nicole with its purpose. "I want to see her."

"Tomorrow." Nicole had folded her arms, rubbing them as though she were cold. Her usually straight posture seemed weighted with more than guilt, and Jake could see physical exhaustion under the strain of their encounter. "She's been asleep for hours."

He saw, too, the shadows behind the clear green of her eyes. Despite the shadows, her eyes still reminded him of leaves in spring. She had come into his life like a spring fairy, bewitching him with the spell of those eyes. She'd left during the same season, leaving him as dazed as any of the mythical victims he'd read about as a child.

"Jake?" Nicole touched his arm, "Before you meet her there's something you should know."

The apology in her expression and the way her teeth chewed at her lower lip put his defenses on alert. He remembered their parting argument too well, and he was sure he knew what she intended to say. "Don't try to tell me she's not mine, Nicki. I won't believe you this time. I know I was your only lover."

She winced, and he knew she remembered as clearly as he the taunted challenge that had made him slam out of the apartment they'd shared.

"Of course she's yours. Even if I'd have denied it in court, there'd have been no doubt once she was born." Her hand on his arm tightened as though to prepare him. "Brianna had meningitis when she was a year old."

Jake tasted the metallic flavor of fear and his gut cramped as though he'd been poleaxed.

"It affected her hearing, Jake." Nicole looked away, then back. "Bri is deaf."

Jake stared at her, unable to respond as he grappled with another shock. *Deaf?* His daughter couldn't be deaf. *His daughter.* The two realities tumbled through his mind, fought for some harbor of acceptance, and found none. No! Not his child.

Jake's face paled beneath his tan, and he moved his head with unconscious denial. Nicole understood his automatic refusal to believe the impossible—but it wasn't impossible because it was true. Jake looked like a fighter struggling through a particularly brutal round, his eyes glazed and his face a blank mask. He had suffered more blows than he could absorb in such a short time. Even though she had buried her worst memories of that time, Nicole had to tell him everything before he would believe in the promise of Brianna's future.

"Why didn't you tell me?"

"That she had meningitis?" Nicole let a fleeting, ironic smile touch her lips. "It would have seemed a little odd, don't you think, since you didn't even know she existed."

Anger flared in his eyes, blue flames of furious heat. "And whose fault was that?" he demanded, his voice raw with controlled rage. "Brianna is mine, too. You had no right to keep her from me—"

"Maybe not," Nicole fired back, "but I didn't know any other way out." His face tightened still more, but he stood rigid and silent while she explained. "By the time she got sick you'd just made the charts with your first record. What do you think would have happened if I'd called to tell you your baby was in the hospital? Do you really think you would have taken my call in the first place, let alone believed me?" Her hand moved to stroke his forearm, unconsciously trying to soothe him. She felt the tightly controlled muscles contract beneath her touch, though he didn't pull away. She wondered if he even felt her.

"When I left, you thought I only cared about myself. Myself and my career and financial success. You'd have thought I was after your money. You wouldn't have accepted a phone call from me in the first place, let alone believed in a baby that I wasn't supposed to have."

"You should have at least given me the chance," Jake retorted. "I wouldn't have denied her then any more than I do now." His eyes blazed with icy blue fire and Nicole recognized the fury and pained betrayal they revealed.

Nicole's throat tightened. Jake didn't deserve the pain she'd given him. They were both responsible for Brianna, but Nicole had made the decision to lie, to leave, and to keep her secret. Her pride had demanded that she take full responsibility for that decision. She couldn't have asked him for help any more than she'd been able to marry him just because she was pregnant.

He would have given up his dreams in order to support Brianna, and Nicole knew she couldn't have lived with that, either. It was another reason why she had left. He had too much talent and she had too much pride.

"I know I hurt you, Jake. I never wanted to, but I had to do what I thought was best for all of us. The reasons might not matter now . . . but they did then."

Jake struggled to maintain his balance in the emotional flood that threatened to overwhelm him as nothing in his life had ever done before. His throat burned with the parched residue of his fury. His eyes and nose stung with the acid of his frustration. He despised the role he might have played in such a scenario.

Honesty made him acknowledge that at the time of his baby's illness he still resented Nicole's rejection enough that he would probably have refused her phone call . . . and he would have trashed a letter without opening it. To know that his refusal would have forever closed the door to his searching for the truth tore him apart. His haunted dreams had held only a fraction of the searing pain of the nightmare he'd just walked into.

A small pocket of warmth on his arm made him look down to where Nicole's hand still rested. He blinked to clear his vision, then looked up to see concern and guilt in Nicole's delicate face. The heat of anger and desire pulled him from the dark well of shock and slammed him into a wall of frustration.

Suddenly he had to move. He had to get away and sort out all the fragments of the last hour's shocks. Adrenaline pumped through him, trying to find escape, and he couldn't stand still any longer.

"I'll be back tomorrow," he said abruptly, then turned quickly away and strode to the door.

Once in his car, Jake gripped the steering wheel until his knuckles gleamed whitely in the faint glow of the streetlight beside the curb. The tiny muscle at his jaw twitched reflexively as he clamped his teeth together to keep from shouting in fury, frustration, and pain.

Damn!

Nothing in his life had prepared him for the roller coaster ride of confrontation, guilt, resentment, denial, euphoria and despair he'd been through in little more than an hour. In his quest for an end to his nagging questions, he'd found answers he'd never considered. He'd even found questions that he didn't want to ask . . . but he knew he would have to find those answers, too.

He forced himself to loosen his death-grip on the steering wheel, then leaned back, trying to ease the tremors that made his body pulse with adrenaline.

* * *

For several minutes after Jake's footsteps had faded out of hearing, Nicole stared after him. Just the sight of him in the doorway when she turned around tonight had been so like the night they met. That night, too, she had looked up to see those vibrant blue eyes watching her every move.

The cast party had been in full swing, as everyone congratulated each other on a job well done. Her partner in the *pas de deux,* David Cole, had gone to get them both a glass of champagne when she looked up to see Jake leaning against the doorway. His heated gaze warmed her whole body and his appreciative smile made her pulse race. He knew she'd seen him, and he gave her a thumbs-up sign of approval.

David had returned just then, and when she glanced over to the doorway a few minutes later, Jake was gone. A flash of disappointment surprised her. She didn't know him, but something about him struck a chord, and she'd looked around to see where he'd gone. He stood at the corner of the room with the members of the small combo that the artistic director, Adam Chambers, had hired for the evening. While she watched, Jake had slipped the broad strap of a guitar over his shoulder and approached the microphone. The others took up their places around him. At his signal they began playing a dance-tempo ballad.

She didn't recognize the song, but the words and melody pulled at her. She danced with David, but her mind centered on the loving tenderness of the music. When it ended, she looked back at the blue-eyed stranger, and knew he'd written it. She knew, too, that he'd played the song because of her. At the end of the set he'd introduced himself, and before the party ended she had agreed to a movie date the next afternoon. A movie date. Nicole grimaced at the irony. What a common beginning for the chaos it tumbled her into.

The loud rumble of a diesel truck floated up from the street below, and Nicole began locking the studio for the night. With everything secured, and all the lights off but one, she walked across the broad expanse of oak floor and climbed the ballroom stairs to the back entrance of her apartment. At the top of the stairs, she flipped a switch and left the ballroom in darkness.

Inside, the dim light of two old-fashioned wall sconces lit her way past the small round dining set into the living room. Maggie, her neighbor, babysitter and receptionist, dozed in the chair.

Schooling her features into their usual expression, Nicole gently woke the older woman. Maggie assured her that Brianna still slept soundly, then let herself out of the apartment to go to her own quarters down the hall.

After securing the door, Nicole headed for the kitchen. Her movements were as mechanical as they were economical while she located a mug, then used a stool to reach deep into the cupboard over the refrigerator to pull out a dusty, half-empty bottle of rum left over from some party. With meticulous care, she made herself a strong hot toddy and carried it back into the living room.

For once the stately, pale blue room failed to soothe her troubled emotions. With a sigh, she sat on the couch that faced the French doors that opened onto the balcony above the ballroom. Her hands trembled, and she set the mug on the low table in front of the couch.

Dear God, why?

She still loved him. Standing in the lobby, watching her words tear him apart, she'd wanted to pull him into her arms and comfort him, to make the hurt go away. She wanted to— She dropped her head back against the cushions and admitted the truth.

Face it. You wanted to make love to him like you never left him. Her body still reacted to his presence, anticipating even an accidental touch. Even more, she wanted his conscious touch. She wanted to feel the texture of his skin, the warmth of his mouth. She wanted to hear his teasing laughter when he pulled her to him.

Nicole sat up straight. *Stop it!* No matter what her body and soul wanted, that would never happen again. If he hadn't hated her five years ago, he did now. She'd seen it in his eyes just before he left. Yet she still couldn't think of any other course she could have followed. Like a dancer out of sync, she knew that if she had accepted Jake's offer of marriage, they would have been no better off . . . and Brianna would have paid the price of their mistake.

A yawn caught her, and she knew she needed to get some rest before the next day. She would need all her strength for Jake's return. Picking up the toddy, she took a single sip, then grimaced. She returned the cup to the kitchen where she poured the rest down the sink. It would take more than false courage to get through tomorrow.

After washing up in the tiny bathroom, she entered the bedroom she shared with her daughter. A faint nightlight glowed, illuminating Brianna's sleeping form. Nicole smiled tenderly as she readjusted the blankets Brianna had kicked off in her sleep. Bending down, she picked up the floppy velveteen rabbit that had been loved as bare of plush as the one in Brianna's favorite story.

Gently, she smoothed the dark curls that surrounded the cherub face. Delicate lids, edged with thick black lashes, covered eyes as brilliant blue as her father's—and just as haunting. She yawned again, then moved to her own bed, slipping out of her leotard and tights before crawling between the sheets.

Jake was making love to her again. Nicole felt the guitar-callused tips of his fingers slowly stroke her skin with the sensuous thoroughness that shortened her breath to gasps of pleasure. His warm mouth teased her throat, nibbling at the sensitive area below her ear, then worked slowly, deliciously down until he captured the waiting rose tips of her breasts.

Heat flashed through her at his touch and his name formed on her lips as she pulled him closer, savoring the sensations his mouth created. His body pressed against her, its hard contours making her hands ache to feel the taut muscles of his flesh. But when she reached for him she touched cloth instead. She tried to brush it aside, to taste the skin underneath. Frustrated and impatient, she tugged at the offending barrier, but it refused to move. She wanted to see him, to revel in the sight of his body just as he was taking delight in hers, but she couldn't open her eyes. With an effort of will, she forced her eyes open and nearly cried out when she realized it was only a dream. Or was it a nightmare?

She sat up, her body still flushed and pulsing from the realness of it, and ruefully told herself it was her own fault for sleeping nude for the first time in years. The fall night air cooled her bare skin, and she forced herself to cross the floor to the dresser. Quickly, she pulled out an old-fashioned, high-necked, flannel nightgown. Back in bed, she forced her dream images away before exhaustion claimed her once more.

Nicole awakened with a start when a small body clambered onto her bed. She scrunched her eyes tightly shut and brought her hands up to sign, "Don't bother me. I'm sleeping."

Brianna, now straddling her mother's middle, chuckled and began to bounce up and down. Nicole quickly sat up in protest, her eyes wide open, then turned the tables on her daughter by tipping her back to tickle her. Brianna giggled in delight as she squirmed out of reach and scrambled to the floor. Nicole flopped back against the pale green sheets just before brilliant blue eyes peeked up over the edge of the bed.

"Eeee!" Brianna pronounced determinedly, the fingers of one hand held close together and gesturing to her mouth. The soft pink blanket sleepers accented her rosy cheeks and lips, and when she smiled, her father's dimples appeared to underscore the flashes of Jake's personality that sparkled from her eyes.

Oh, Jake, why did you have to come looking for answers? But he had, and crying about it wouldn't solve anything. She smiled at Brianna, determined to face today the same as any other. "Okay, imp, I'll feed you." She swung her feet over the edge of the bed and took Brianna's hand as she stood up. Her other hand moved quickly as she asked, "Do you want eggs or cereal?"

"Eggs," Brianna signed, "and bacon."

Nicole stopped and faced her daughter. "What?" her hands asked. "I didn't hear you."

Brianna's sunny expression clouded for a moment, then returned to its usual good humor. *"Aigh-a-baiik,"* she repeated patiently.

"Ba-cannn," Nicole laid her hand beside her nose as she emphasized the "n" sound.

Obediently, Brianna put her small hand beside her own nose as she repeated, *"Baiikann."*

"Very good!" Nicole scooped Brianna into her arms and hugged her fiercely. When Brianna squirmed to get down, Nicole let her, then signed, "I love you."

Brianna laughed and ran into the kitchen to wait for her breakfast.

"Okay, everybody, let's try it again," Nicole encouraged the girls who stood around her, panting from their exertions. Her body was damp from leading them through the intricate steps of the Nutcracker ballet's second act snow scene. She stopped to remove the thick pink leg warmers she had worn while warming up and demonstrating the walk through of the steps. "Remember to keep together and watch your line. Real snowflakes may be unique, but dancing ones are supposed to move together."

She turned to face the long mirrors that lined the inside wall and watched her twelve advanced students arrange themselves into formation again. It had been a hectic morning, with an early rehearsal for the opening party scene, and now with the Dance of the Snowflakes. Wondering when Jake would arrive didn't help the tension any, either. Nor had the whispered supposition from her older students who had been in class the night before.

She would have to say something eventually, she supposed. But what? *Yes, class, the famous Jake Cameron and I were lovers years ago—and by the way, Brianna is his daughter?* Not likely. On the other hand, could she pretend that Brianna didn't reveal her parentage by her very looks and actions? She had never claimed Brianna was legitimate, but neither had Nicole corrected the assumption she was divorced.

The girls waited, poised in formation, and she began calling the steps and moving with them. "Now, together—and . . . file into position . . . *pique releve* and . . . *enchainment* . . . little steps, little steps—stay in place. Right! Now start moving your arms. Less angle in the elbows, Carol. Good, that's better." She continued chanting the sequence, though she had stopped moving with them and turned to keep a more watchful eye on their movements. When they completed the run through, Nicole said, "Now, let's see if you can do it to music."

She moved briskly to the tape recorder beside the record player stand. She punched the rewind button, and as the counter spun backward to the beginning of the scene's music she glanced at her watch. 1:30. Not bad for an hour and a half of rehearsal this early into production. If they maintained this rate they might have the whole scene blocked out by two o'clock.

Her gaze strayed to the lobby, but it was still empty. Jake said he'd be back, but he hadn't said when. The not knowing made her jumpy. She had to fight to keep her usual light banter from becoming terse.

The automatic stop on the recorder clicked, and she called, "Starting positions." She watched them come to attention, smiling when a few groaned. "Hey, this is the hardest part, you know. Once you get past the memorization, it's simple sweat and pain the rest of the way."

When she saw they were ready, she started the music. They stood at each of the far corners of the ballroom, arms held rounded at their sides, toes pointed in readiness to file to the center of the floor. The regal gracefulness of their poses struck an incongruous note with the odd mixture of practice costumes. Wearing plastic sweat bloomers, sweatshirts tied at the waist with elastic, ragged leg warmers, and mismatched leotards and tights, they contrasted strikingly from Nicole's mental image of the flowing white chiffon and sparkling silver trim of the costumes they would wear during the performance.

They were in the middle of the final movements—three rows of four dancers, hands fluttering lightly as they raised and lowered their arms in unison—when Nicole felt Jake's presence behind her. She had hoped he would arrive after the girls left, but she knew without turning around that he was there.

Two

The girls finished the dance, holding the final pose for a moment, then Nicole stopped the music and they all relaxed, trying to slow their rapid breathing. Nicole turned then and told Jake, "I'm almost finished."

He nodded his head. "No problem."

Nicole's glance took in the lean lines of Jake's body, and a wave of sensual warmth washed over her. She knew every inch of that torso, the powerful arms, those long legs. She breathed in sharply and smelled the faint musk that reminded her of her dream. It was her memory working overtime, since they were too far apart for it to be real. Only Jake could send phantom scents through her soul.

She felt awkward and uncomfortable in the thin dance clothes she wore like a uniform. She was covered from neck to toe, but the clinging fabric she never thought about at any other time now seemed bent on betraying her as the plum colored leotard revealed the tightening of her body.

Nicole forced her attention back to the dancers who stretched and flexed their muscles in relaxation exercises. Kristen had followed Nicole's earlier example and removed her leg warmers, and Sharon retied her toe shoes. They went through the sequence three more times, and then Nicole dismissed them.

"That should do it for today, girls. Don't forget that Bonnie wants to fit your costumes Monday night before class. Try to get here early."

Jake stepped back, giving the girls room to pass. A few smiled shyly at him as they filed out, and he nodded in vague acknowledgment. Their combined scents: youthful floral, sweat, and rosin, brought back the sharp memories of picking Nicole up after rehearsals. He crossed the threshold into the practice room and was assailed by the sting of crushed rosin and dusty velvet mingled with glass cleaner, lingering female bouquet . . . and Nicki. Her presence labeled the room as her domain in a way he couldn't name. She didn't wear the same perfume she'd worn when they were together, but he could have walked into this room anytime and felt her closeness.

As she had the night before, Nicole rearranged records and tapes. Her fingers fumbled as she slid a record into its jacket, and he felt a ripple of satisfaction when he realized she was as nervous as he was. He didn't like the unease that had riddled his fitful sleep or the sudden wash of heat and cold that electrified his body whenever he thought about meeting his child for the first time.

His child. The words still sounded like something from a song lyric rather than reality. His imagination tried to supply him with an image but failed. She would have dark hair, but did her eyes sparkle with the glow of emeralds or sapphires? Did she have the light fairy grace and lilting laughter of her mother?

What about her deafness? He remembered something on television a while back about new surgical methods that restored hearing. Had Nicole checked on it? He focused on Nicole, then glanced at the almost empty foyer. Of course she had. Nicole would be as protective of her child as a tigress. She would sell her soul before she would ignore a chance to help her child be normal.

He saw her check the foyer, then shift one more album as the last two students crossed the room and started down the stairs.

"My apartment is upstairs," Nicole said when they'd gone. She didn't wait for him to answer but led the way to the back entrance at the far end of the studio.

As she climbed toward her apartment, Jake tried to think of something casual to say, something to ease the added tension that had sprung up when she'd turned to face him. The stirring air carried her faint fragrance and triggered the flash of an erotic dream. A charge of desire lanced through his body and rendered him silent.

They reached the top of the stairs before Nicole spoke. "Brianna's taking her nap, but she should wake soon."

Inside, Nicole introduced Jake to the elderly neighbor who had watched Brianna during the rehearsal. Nicole's presence might be notable in the studio, but her essence filled her apartment. The furniture reflected uncluttered lines softened by rich fabrics in soothing colors. The entertainment center against the wall held a cluster of photographs, and he was tempted to inspect them, looking for clues to her life without him.

When Maggie left, Nicole gestured toward the couch. "Why don't you sit down while I change?"

He knew she'd read his heated thoughts and that he'd made her aware of herself. He couldn't tear his eyes away from the fascinating sight of her nipples hardening beneath the revealing cloth. A faint flush warmed the skin above the neckline of her leotard before she turned away, and started quickly toward a door.

Jake suddenly realized that his daughter slept nearby.

"Nicki?" He cleared his throat, disgusted with the husky uncertainty it revealed. "I know she's asleep, but if I promise not to wake her . . . ?"

Nicole opened the door and Jake saw it was the bathroom, not a bedroom. She indicated another door across the hall. "Go on in, Jake, she won't wake up until she is ready."

The bathroom door shut behind her, and Jake gathered his courage. When he left the night before it had taken nearly an hour before he felt in control enough to make the sixty-mile drive home to Los Angeles. Once there, he considered getting roaring drunk, but the times past when he'd used liquor to numb his senses, the result had been an aching head with which to face the problems that still needed to be solved. And it hadn't changed the fact that Nicole had left him. That night was still burned into his memory, even though the alcohol he'd consumed left his head throbbing for two days.

Instead, he spent last night listening to recordings of the songs he'd written in his pain and anger. He listened to them in the order of their composition, and he heard the slow growth from blind rage to what he'd thought was recovery. When he'd first looked through the glass doors to the studio he'd believed his interview with Nicole would be the final closure to their affair. He'd figured he would satisfy himself that she was as cold and hard as he pictured her. Maybe he'd write his last memory song and go on with his life. But nothing had been as he'd expected.

The sound of the shower reminded him that Nicole would be out soon, and he moved quietly to the bedroom door. He hesitated an instant before turning the knob, chiding himself for the dampness that coated his palms. He hadn't felt stage fright for years, but his pounding heart and shortness of breath threatened to suffocate him if he didn't open the door.

Against the far wall, her bed tumbled with stuffed animals, Brianna lay curled around her pillow. All his blank imaginings became a picture filled with the rightness of reality, and the chill pounding of his heart was replaced by a flood of warmth and awe.

Sun-bright brown hair that would deepen to the rich cinnamon darkness of Nicole's clung to her cheeks and spread across the blankets. Jake swallowed, his throat closing tightly. He blinked quickly to clear the sudden moisture that blurred his vision. God, she was so little . . . she was so big. *My baby.* How much had he missed? First smiles, first teeth, first steps. . . .

Never had Jake felt as unsure of how to proceed as he did now. How did a man make up for missing all those firsts? When he'd found out Nicole was pregnant he'd accepted the responsibility for his actions, but he'd never understood what those responsibilities really meant. He wouldn't have considered deserting Nicole when she was "in trouble," but he hadn't once thought about the needs of a child. His child.

What now? He looked down at the sweet face that slept in innocence and felt a welling of protective tenderness. If Nicole hadn't named him on the birth certificate, he would adopt Brianna legally. Then he would do everything in his power to make sure he missed no more firsts.

It wouldn't be easy. He couldn't exactly change his life as easily as he might have five years ago. At that point in his life the change from aspiring singer to everyday working man would have involved no one but himself. Now he had a full complement of technical staff as well as a public who expected to see him in person as a return for buying his albums.

Financially, he could afford to cut back his schedule, but most of his tours had been booked more than a year in advance. It would be close to two years before any cutbacks made an impact on his time schedule. Still, Nicole and Brianna could travel with him until she started school. Later, they could hire a tutor. . . .

Brianna sighed softly in her sleep, then rolled over onto her stomach, burrowing her face into the pillow. He reached out to brush the dark tendrils away from her face but checked his impulse. He didn't want her to awaken before Nicole was with him. He put his hands in his pockets to prevent himself from touching her, from gathering her into his arms and reassuring himself that she was real. He was a stranger, and he didn't want to frighten her.

The shower shut off, and a few minutes later Nicole stood in the doorway wearing a thick white robe, her feet bare. Jake looked up and forced his vocal cords to work, wincing at the raw sound they made.

"She looks like you."

"She has your eyes."

They looked at each other, neither of them able to say more. Brianna shifted in her sleep and Nicole said, "Maybe you'd better go back into the living room. I'll be with you in a few minutes."

When Nicole returned, now dressed in worn jeans and a bulky green sweater, and offered him iced tea, he declined. He couldn't swallow the lump in his throat, let alone anything else.

He took a seat at the end of the couch. She sat in the chair across from it. Silence held them again.

"Jake—"

"Nicki—"

They both broke the silence at the same time, then Nicole gestured for Jake to continue. Fragmented questions crowded inside his head, none of them able to take sensible form. He settled on the only one that could.

"Why?" He cleared his throat and tried to clear his mind as well. "Why did you lie to me, Nicki?"

"Because I didn't know what else to do."

"But I offered to marry you—"

"Yes . . . and that's why I had to lie."

"Even if you hadn't married me I would have taken care of you," he argued.

"I know, and it would have destroyed us both."

Jake ran his fingers through his hair, frustration eating at him. "That doesn't make any sense—"

"You would have ended up hating me just as surely as you do now. I would have felt guilty, and Brianna would have been caught in the middle of it."

"Don't be ridiculous." Jake felt his uncertainty evaporate in a flash of irritation. "I might have hated you that night, but what did you expect when you first refused to marry me and then threatened to name someone else as the father?" Jake sat back against the cushions and pinned Nicole with a challenging look that belied the regret in his words. "I shouldn't have told you to leave, Nicole. I knew the baby couldn't be anyone's but mine."

"I would have left anyway. I couldn't stay after telling you what I did."

Jake studied her as she sat across from him, her feet tucked up under her, her arms clasped around her knees. How many afternoons had he watched her sit like that, curled up like a child while they talked or watched television? The feelings she drew from him weren't childlike then . . . nor were they now. His sense of betrayal warred with his instinctive desire for her. Nicole's curious blend of delicate softness and tough strength mesmerized him at the same time as it fired his imagination and stirred his body. Annoyed with himself for letting his mind stray, he looked away.

"Where did you go?" he asked. "When I came home and your things were gone, I went to Adam's studio, but neither he nor David would tell me anything. Did you go home to your parents?"

"No, I didn't go home." Nicole smiled without amusement. "You can never go home again. Didn't you know that? Even if you want to, and I didn't." She turned to look at him, her eyes shadowed with memories. "There's no point in putting ourselves through the might-have-beens, Jake. Let's concentrate on the present."

"Not until you tell me about Brianna."

"She's the one thing I don't regret." Nicole's face lost its tightness, her eyes lighting with pleasure when she thought of her daughter. "Don't ever think of her as a mistake, no matter how unplanned she was. Miracles are never mistakes."

"What about her hearing?"

"That's part of the miracle she is. I almost lost her." The green in her eyes darkened with pain; then she shook her head and took a deep breath.

"There's not much to tell. One afternoon she slept later than usual, and when I went in to check on her, she was lying in bed awake but listless. I thought she might be cutting a tooth, but later, when she started throwing up and the fever jumped, I brought her to the emergency room at the hospital. They took her into an examining room and made me go to the waiting room while they checked her."

Nicole closed her eyes, remembering the terrible wait. "After three hours without a word, the doctor finally came out and told me she'd had convulsions and was partially paralyzed, but they thought it would be temporary. He was waiting for test results, but he was sure it was meningitis. He told me all about the possible complications, but none of it sank in. I was just so grateful she was alive I didn't care about anything else."

Nicole shrugged her shoulders. "In the end, that's what counted. I learned sign language and put her into the county deaf program as soon as she was old enough. Now she is just as healthy and happy as any other four-year-old. She doesn't remember life before deafness, so she doesn't miss it."

Jake sat without moving for several minutes, and Nicole waited for him to say something. When he did, he shocked her.

"Marry me, Nicki. I'll adopt Brianna and give her a name."

Nicole stiffened. "What do you mean, give her a name?" Ice replaced the warmth that had lit her eyes, her voice as cold as her stare. "Brianna has a name. It is on her birth certificate. The days are long past when a woman has to marry in order to have a place in society or for her child to have worth."

"That's not what I meant." Jake felt his temper rising. "Damn it, I want to really be her father—not some biological accident of accountability."

"You're not accountable, Jake. Brianna was my choice; she's my responsibility. I could have had the abortion."

"I know that." Jake controlled his desire to shout at her. "You made that clear the night you left." He ran his hand through his hair in frustration. "I want to be a part of her life. I've missed too much of it already."

"We don't have to get married for you to do that."

"You mean you'll let me have visiting rights?" he asked with menacing softness. Heat simmered in his belly, tempering the steel of his resolution and sharpening the edge of his fury. "You mean I can be a weekend father, like we were divorced and I lost?"

He gave a harsh laugh, and the sound of it made Nicole flinch. "I've seen how that works out. Half the musicians I know are divorced fathers. They're like little kids looking over the fence at a birthday party—able to watch what's happening, but never really a part of the fun."

"Marriages can be like that, too."

Her voice held a note of conviction that pulled Jake's anger back and made him watch her warily. She sat up, letting her feet touch the floor and straightening with unconscious dignity. "I'm giving you an invitation to the party, Jake. If you stay on the other side of the fence just because you can't be the one to cut the cake, it's your fault, not mine."

Even though his fury no longer threatened his control, enough still lapped at his nerve endings to make him want to shake her cool conviction.

"There's one thing you're forgetting, Nicki."

"What's that?"

"I'm not just plain Jake Cameron now. When people find out I'm Brianna's father, the press will make your life hell. They love stories about former girlfriends and illegitimate kids. If we're married and I adopt Brianna, she'll be less of a target."

Fear clutched Nicole as Jake spoke. She hadn't thought about the public side of his life, though she was sure he was wrong. If the press found out about Brianna it would be a ninety-day wonder. Then they would find another story, just as juicy and as capable of selling papers.

"No." She met Jake's burning gaze with cool deliberation. "You can't scare me into doing what you want, either. We'll work out a way for you to be a part of Brianna's life, but marriage isn't the way. I won't marry you or anyone else just to give Brianna a father."

"What about you? What do you want out of marriage?"

"I want more than obligation and convenience," she retorted.

"Is that what you think I mean? Some kind of Victorian marriage of convenience?" Jake's harsh laugh grated against Nicole's ears. "I promise you our marriage would be real in every sense. We couldn't live together and not be lovers. That's how Brianna happened, remember?"

He leaned across the short distance between them, his voice softening as he captured her hand. "You couldn't have forgotten any more than I have," he said. He laid her palm against his lips, his breath warming it before he flicked his tongue lightly over the base of her thumb. Shimmering fingers of heat raced through her.

He tugged, urging her out of the chair and closer to him. "I still wake up nights with the taste of you in my fading dream." His lips touched her wrist, and her pulse surged with anticipation. "I remember the little kitten sounds you made when I touched you, the way you moved against me, driving me insane with your softness."

He moved to meet her, pulling her down onto the couch and his hand cupping her face with gentle persuasion. She caught the never-forgotten pleasure of his scent as his thumb grazed her mouth. "Kiss me, Nicki," he whispered. "Let me see if my dream memories are like the real thing."

Nicole wanted to deny the lulling tug of Jake's words, to resist the slow pull of his hands as they drew her closer to him, but even more, she wanted to give in, to kiss him as he asked . . . to compare her dreams to his.

He leaned toward her, tantalizing her with lightly coaxing kisses, and she gave in to the pleasure of his mouth. His moustache teased her as it brushed against her cheek, his lips firm and warm beneath its feathery softness. Her hand reached up, smoothing his face and beard, then slipped around to tangle in the silky hair at the back of his neck. It set off memories of other times—times when its finely textured richness lay pressed to her breast, while they recovered from hours of lovemaking that had taken them beyond reason.

Her hands slid down, kneading the taut muscles of his back and arms, discovering new volume, greater corded mass, where before there had been sinewy leanness. Jake lightly traced her lips, his tongue leaving a damp trail, and her mouth softened, turning to meet it. He tasted like winter nights warmed by desire, and Nicole murmured his name before returning his heady invasion.

Deep within her, embers of need glowed, their heat coiling up through her body, making her curl close to him, wanting him to carry the magic further. When his arms gathered her tightly to him, his hands sliding the length of her back, stroking and caressing, the embers kindled, and the sparks lit emotions Nicole thought long buried.

Jake felt Nicole press against him, her hands urging him to taste the honeyed recesses of her mouth, and he groaned in response. Hot, sweet, and inviting, the tender interior was his to explore. When she whispered his name, then answered his questing mouth by taking his tongue fully and deeply, he crushed her to him, wanting to capture her soul as they shared the same breath.

Jake finally released her mouth, then pressed tiny, nibbling kisses along her jaw, easing up to her ear. "It's been so long, Nicki," he murmured as he teased the lobe. "Too long."

She shivered, then tipped her head to give him access to the soft skin of her neck. He let his tongue slide along the slender column, savoring the smoothness of her flesh beneath his damp caress. He raised his head to taste her lips again, his pulse pounding at the sight of their swollen invitation, when a movement behind the couch caught his attention. He stiffened, drawing away from Nicole, his heated emotions cooling quickly.

Nicole felt Jake's withdrawal and protested, her voice as bewildered as it was husky. "Jake?"

She opened her eyes to see his gaze focused beyond the couch. *Brianna.* Quickly she straightened, self-consciously smoothing her hair into the coil at the back of her head before turning toward her daughter.

Brianna stared wide-eyed at the bearded giant who had risen from the couch. When she saw Nicole stand up as well, her wariness melted and curiosity took over. Her hand moved to touch her thumb to her chin while the index finger wiggled in and out above her small fist.

Nicole hesitated a minute, then faced her palm toward Brianna.

She spread her fingers and shifted her hand until the thumb touched her forehead.

"She wants to know who you are," she translated for Jake. She turned to him, speaking calmly despite the passion that had raged within her moments before. "I told her that you're her father."

Jake felt his heart splinter, shards of joy piercing his soul. His eyes stung with emotion. "Thank you for that, Nicki."

He looked back to Brianna, and warmth spread through him. Nicki was right. Brianna's serious inspection revealed eyes as blue as his with the same dark ring defining the edge of the iris.

Brianna studied him, then walked to the console against the far wall. When she opened the storage door below the CD player and sorted through the discs inside, Nicole gave a small gasp of surprise.

"What's she doing?" Jake asked.

Nicole's eyes misted and she had to clear her throat of emotion before she could answer. "She's looking for one of your albums." They both sat back down on the couch. "When she was first learning family signs I showed her your picture and told her it was Daddy, but since it was just a picture, I was never sure if she understood."

Jake felt winded, as though he'd been running long distances uphill. Since Nicole had confirmed that he was a father who had lost the first four years of his daughter's life, little demons of anger had been prodding him, the pain catching him whenever his guard was down. Knowing that Nicole had given Brianna some link with him, even one so vague and tenuous as a picture on an album cover, softened the sharp edge of his loss.

Brianna returned to the front of the couch and studied Jake's face against the cover image with the rakish grin.

"Try smiling at her," Nicole said.

Jake gave Brianna a tentative smile that grew to a grin when Brianna answered with a shy smile of her own. She repeated Nicole's spread-fingered sign, then put the album on the low coffee table. Her hands moved quickly, her tiny fingers blurring in her haste.

"Hey, slow down." Nicole laughed. Just knowing Brianna had made the connection and accepted Jake as her father made Nicole's spirits soar.

She watched Brianna's questioning hands as she continued translating for Jake. "She wants to know where you've been, why you're here now, and—" she hesitated, then resolutely went on, "if you're going to live with us like Jenny's father. She means he lives with Jenny," Nicole clarified. She signed to Brianna, answering aloud at the same time. "No, Daddy will live at his own house, like Michael's daddy."

Jake murmured, "Nicki—"

"No." Nicole flashed him a warning glance. "Don't push it."

Jake sat only inches away, but Nicole knew he felt isolated from them, separated by a gulf of communication and a canyon of time. She could think of nothing to ease the tight line of tension around his mouth or the hurt, half angry light in his eyes.

Satisfied with Nicole's explanations, Brianna pointed her finger to herself, then moved the same finger to touch her lower jaw, twisting it back and forth in short quick movements.

"She wants a piece of candy." Nicole chuckled. "She still has a few pieces from Halloween, and I let her have a piece after her nap. I'll be right back." Glad for the excuse to move, Nicole went into the kitchen. Her relief was short-lived, however, when Jake followed her. There was too little space in the tiny kitchen and his presence filled it, making Nicole more aware of him than before.

"Which cupboard is it in?" he asked when she started to get out the small stool in the corner.

"The one on the left, top shelf. But she won't take it from you. I've taught her never to—" Nicole broke off as she realized how painful the words were. "Jake, I'm sorry, I didn't mean to—"

"Drop it!" he ordered shortly. He held the nearly empty brown sack of candy out to her.

Nicole automatically thanked him before kneeling down and opening the bag for Brianna to make her choice. All that remained were a green lollipop, two Tootsie Rolls, and a cellophane-wrapped piece of butterscotch. Brianna deliberated carefully before finally reaching for the lollipop. Then, before Nicole could close the bag, Brianna's other hand quickly secured the butterscotch and offered it to Jake.

"Thank you, Brianna." His chest ached with pride and a rush of love that threatened to overwhelm him. He knelt, holding his arms out to her, but she wasn't yet ready to hug him. She giggled shyly before running back to the living room.

"Try to be patient, Jake," Nicole whispered as he dropped his arms and stood again. "It'll come in time."

"I hope so."

Big Bird and Maria of Sesame Street were singing a song when Nicole and Jake reentered the living room. Brianna sat before the television screen, the lollipop held firmly in an already sticky fist as she watched intently.

"Can she read lips?" Jake asked.

"She's learning," Nicole sat on the chair opposite the couch again. She needed space between them after the interlude before. "It takes a while but she's doing very well for her age. She especially likes this show, though, because one of the cast members is deaf, and they use sign language a lot. She can follow more of what is happening."

"Did she understand me when I thanked her?" Jake held the bright yellow candy, unconsciously playing with the twisted ends of the cellophane.

"She understood your meaning," Nicole hedged. She didn't want to add to his pain, but he caught the slight hesitation in her tone.

"Meaning?"

Knowing he would persist until she told him, Nicole tried to soften her words. "Reading lips is very difficult, even for an adult. When a child or an adult meets someone new they are often unsure of the person, and it affects their concentration on what is being said. It's even harder if the speaker doesn't move his lips, or covers them with his hands . . . or has a moustache or beard."

Jake smoothed the hair from his mouth as what Nicole was saying became clear. "I see."

Nicole didn't want to add to Jake's frustration at being a stranger to his own child, but she also knew she had to be totally honest with him. "It will also take a while before she'll speak in front of you."

"You mean she can talk?"

"Oh, yes," Nicole assured him. "But her words aren't as clear as a child who can hear. She tried speaking to other people for a while, but their expressions told her that they not only didn't know what she was saying, but that her speech was unpleasant to them."

Nicole looked over to where Brianna was still engrossed in the television program. "She's become very wary of using her voice in front of other people. I know I should make her speak as often as possible—I do when we're alone—but . . ."

Nicole searched her mind for something to ease the uncomfortable silence that followed when they heard a short rapping knock on the door by the back stairway.

"Nicole? Hurry up, woman, you're late!" The door opened and Nicole's former dancing partner, David Cole, came in without waiting for an answer. Slightly taller than average, with a muscular grace that spoke of power and control, he started across the room, then caught sight of the man on the couch and stopped.

"My God . . . Jake!"

Three

Silence held them for several seconds, and then Jake acknowledged him with a curt nod. "David."

Nicole jumped up and started toward David, then stopped. "Oh, Lord. I forgot about our rehearsal! What time is it?"

David still gaped at Jake, his hazel eyes focused on the two of them.

"A quarter 'til five," Jake answered for him.

The movement by the door had attracted Brianna's attention and, with a squeal of delight, she jumped up and threw herself into David's arms. Brianna's hands spoke rapidly, and the sign Daddy appeared often. David answered her in kind, though more slowly and with less enthusiasm. Finally he put her down, signing for her to watch television again.

Nicole knew she should go change back into her dancing clothes, but she hesitated against leaving Jake and David alone. Jake had never understood her and David's friendship, not able to believe that there was no romantic attachment. He had never fully comprehended that David could be one of her closest friends without the physical involvement of a man and woman. But then, Nicole had never told him about David and Cathy. Cathy had been too fresh a pain, too recent a memory to talk about when she and Jake were lovers.

She had to admit that in the first lonely months after having Brianna, Nicole had considered seeking comfort and companionship with David. It had not taken her long, however, to realize that they could never be lovers. Nonetheless, David was fiercely protective of her, and Nicole could feel the animosity between the two men.

David took a step toward her. "Nicole?"

"It's okay, David," Nicole's green eyes pleaded with him not to argue. "Start warming up, and I'll be down in a few minutes."

He searched her face carefully before giving a nod and disappearing the way he had come.

"Makes himself right at home, doesn't he?"

The quiet fury in Jake's voice made Nicole stiffen defensively, her stomach churning at the insinuation oiling his words. She didn't trust herself to speak.

"And he's certainly no stranger to Brianna, is he? No wonder you have your apartment above the studio. It's so much more convenient."

Nicole refused to listen to anymore. She turned toward the door, striding over to yank it open. "Get out, Jake."

She refused to look at him, her anger killing all the compassion and guilt of moments before. "If you want me to even let you near Brianna again you'll leave right now."

He came to stand in front of her, but she refused the pull of his gaze, his silent battle of will to make her look at him. "Don't come back until you can get your mind out of the gutter."

"Are you sure it's in the gutter, Nicole? Maybe it's just on the right track. As for letting me near Brianna, science has come a long way in determining paternity during the past five years. I'll fight for my rights this time." He stalked past her and down the stairs.

She closed the door after him and leaned against it. Damn the man and his dog-in-the-manger attitude! He didn't really want her, but he didn't want anyone else to have her. And where did he get off condemning her lifestyle? Convenient? Yes, her apartment was convenient. It meant she got to spend odd minutes with Brianna all day. It meant she could be assured that Bri's care was as secure and loving as it should be.

She drew a shuddering breath to control the surging tide of weeping that threatened to drown her. It was a wasted effort. A single tear rolled slowly down her pale cheek. Its twin followed, trying to catch the first.

The telephone rang, and Nicole fought to sound normal as she lifted the receiver.

"Are you okay?" David asked quietly through the line from the lobby phone.

"Yes, I'm fine." Nicole told him. "David . . . did he—?"

"He didn't say anything to me," David reassured her. "He just stormed out with a grim look." Gently, he said, "Look, why don't you finish your cry, and if you want me to stick around . . . to talk or anything, I'll be here. How does that sound to you?"

Nicole gave a watery smile at David's perception. "Thank you, David." Tears gathered again, and her voice wavered, "You always seem to know what I need."

There was an awkward pause before his voice answered gruffly, "Yeah."

Three hours later, Jake opened the door of his Beverly Hills home, tossing a small brown bag onto the table that stood in the entry hall. He looked at his image reflected by the mirror above the table and frowned. He'd made a mess of things. He couldn't blame Nicki for throwing him out of her apartment. He had no right to make disparaging comments about her love life. They weren't married, and according to Nicole they never would be, so why did seeing David walk in as though he belonged in her apartment make Jake seethe with frustrated rage?

Anger had smoldered in him since he'd heard Nicole's voice again and known the fading whisper in his erotic dreams had been her voice . . . always hers. The anger had been there before Brianna climbed into David's arms, letting him hold her when she hadn't let Jake. It was more than the realization that David communicated with Bri naturally and without strain. It was more than the fact that David had obviously been a part of all the "first times" Jake had missed in Brianna's life.

It was seeing the silent communication between David and Nicole. David wouldn't have left if Nicole hadn't signaled for him to. With a single look she had told him she meant what she said. Only a lover should be able to read a woman that well. Was David Nicole's lover now? His stomach churned as the acid of jealousy burned him and left its bitter taste on his tongue.

Jake walked down the long narrow hall that bisected the house. He flipped on the light in the den and set the books he carried onto the bar built into the corner. Damn! He had never understood the bond between them. Even that first night, at the party when he and Nicole met, he'd been aware of the special tie between her and David.

When he saw them perform together on stage a few days later David had moved with her, had held her, with all the passion and sexual communication of the music. Jake had felt a stab of jealous possessiveness to know that another man knew how to make Nicole's body flow with so much fire. Afterward he'd hurried to the dressing areas, sure he would find them locked in an embrace, but the air had been charged with nothing more than first-night exuberance.

They weren't related, nor was David gay. Yet when Jake had asked Nicole about their relationship she had told him David was a special friend and that they'd been through some rough times together. Her explanation had been too vague for his tastes. He'd even expected David to put up some kind of block when Jake started seeing Nicole regularly. But he hadn't. Nor had he seemed especially concerned when Nicole moved in with Jake a month later.

He stepped around the brass-edged counter to lower himself wearily into the leather recliner in the corner. So now what? He needed to sort out his emotions. He had to make plans for Brianna's future. He had to concentrate.

He sat forward and pulled out the drawer under the telephone table beside the chair. He pulled out the pencil and note tablet he kept there and closed the drawer. Sitting back, he closed his eyes and tried to focus. Instead of practical plans of how to deal with the news that he had a daughter, all that passed through his mind was a kaleidoscope of pictures of Nicki while hunger gnawed at his soul.

He'd heard her lilting laughter while setting up his equipment at Adam Chambers' party. It had rippled through him, bringing his senses alert and causing him to pinch his thumb on the hinge of the guitar case when he looked up to see who she was. He saw her dancing with David and decided to claim her for himself. He shook his head, an odd repugnance gripping him as he remembered how calculatingly determined he'd been to get Nicole into his bed.

She had been barely out of high school and innocent in an aware sort of way. As a dancer she had seen plenty of affairs, plenty of the less glamorous side of life in the entertainment world, yet she hadn't succumbed to its influence. He'd known that while he watched her. Yet he'd decided to take that innocence for himself.

He'd always been sure of himself and his goals. Nothing could hold him down. He intended to prove to his father that he could make a living with music, that it wasn't some silly pipe dream that couldn't come true. He firmly believed that the only way to achieve what he wanted was to go after it, no matter what other people thought, no matter what he had to give up to succeed. Of course, at the time he hadn't had to give up much. His parents weren't happy with his choices, but they hadn't disowned him. In fact, his attitude hadn't been tested at all.

When he met Nicole, he focused every spare moment that wasn't required for group rehearsals or band gigs on her. Her schedule suited him. They both had mornings free. In the afternoon they each had rehearsals, and at night she danced or attended classes while he played gigs in the small bars and occasional private parties like the one where they'd met.

It was the ideal life for the swinging would-be star. His own apartment, a desirable live-in girlfriend, and increasingly regular jobs. What more could a twenty-four-year-old cocky fool wish for? A self-mocking smile flitted across his face. Nothing. Then one morning he'd walked into the bathroom and the whole thing had crashed.

Nicole had gone in to take a shower and he'd decided to take her a fresh towel. When he opened the door, Nicole was standing beside the sink in her robe. The steam from the shower's running water stirred in the cool air from the open door and she spun around, dropping the white plastic she held. Jake reached to pick it up, but

Nicole snatched it from the floor and quickly tossed it into the trash.

"You startled me."

Her face was pale despite the warmth from the rising steam and Jake felt his gut clench with suspicion.

"What was that you threw away?"

"Nothing. Just a piece of plastic."

Jake looked beyond her shoulder as she braced herself against the front of the sink. The mirror's reflection confirmed his fear. A home pregnancy test box sat on the counter behind her and her expression told him the results.

The fine hairs on the back of his arms and along his neck had lifted as though sensing danger. In that brief instant he'd felt hunted, trapped, and betrayed. Had she planned to trap him? Had she seduced him until his blood ran hot at the sight of her and made him forget caution . . . precaution?

"So, I guess I'm going to be a father."

"No, you're not." Nicole had turned to face him, her chin held high, her eyes defiant. "I may be pregnant," she said, "but you don't have to worry about a thing."

He'd looked at her and known his response to her was his making, not hers. She'd taken a step back when he'd spoken, though he didn't think she realized she'd made the defensive move. Her eyes had dilated with shock as real as his own. She hadn't planned it, and he couldn't let her face it alone.

"Neither do you." Jake had recovered his senses and knew what he had to do. One thing his parents had instilled in him was that a man faced his responsibilities no matter what the cost. "We'll get married. I'll go into my father's accounting firm. He's always wanted me to."

"No."

"Nicki, a kid needs a father who's home every night. Besides, I couldn't support three of us on what I make with music. I'll get a regular job with a regular paycheck and—"

"I said, no. You aren't giving up music, and I'm not giving up dancing." Nicole's face had become a chalky white, her green eyes glittering with something Jake couldn't name, something that tore at him nearly as much as her next words. "I'll get an abortion."

She must not have understood him. "You don't have to. I'm not without some sense of responsibility. We can get married this afternoon."

"I don't need your responsibility. I'm not marrying you."

Her rigid posture, even as she turned away from the anger that filled him then, convinced him she meant it. Dancing meant more to her than having his baby. Dancing meant more to her than marrying him. He was willing to give up his dreams, but she wouldn't give up hers. White hot pain lanced him, then rage, just as hot, just as searing.

"You can't. Damn it, if you don't want to marry me, fine. I told you when we first met that I didn't plan to get married, but I won't let you—!"

"What do you mean you won't let me? You don't have anything to say about it. We're not married, Jake, and we're not going to be. You can't make me do anything."

"That baby is half mine. You can't—"

"How do you know, Jake?" Nicole threw the words at him, her face still pale and drawn, her stance that of a hunted creature, "Maybe I'll say David is the father. Maybe I'll say I don't know who the father is—"

"Stop it!"

Nicole froze then, and he'd clenched his fists to keep from shaking her in fury. "Don't say another word." His words had been whispered through clenched teeth, clipped and precise. "I want you out of here. You have one week to find a place to stay. I've been offered a gig that will take me out of town until then. When I come back, you better be gone."

He'd slammed out of the apartment, striding down the hall and into the street before he realized he'd moved. He'd gone into the first bar he'd found and ordered a scotch and water. After he'd calmed down, he had known Nicole's taunt had been no more than that. He'd been her first and only lover. How many times had he ignored precautionary measures because he didn't want to wait, didn't want to think when he had Nicki in his arms?

The baby was his, and he was responsible. They would work things out some way. But when he returned to the apartment three hours later she was gone. Nothing remained to show she had ever been there . . . except the terrible emptiness she left behind.

Jake rubbed his throbbing temples. He should take a couple of aspirin, but he doubted if they would be very effective. A few pills couldn't fight his tension, facing the past would. Nicole said she would have left him even if he hadn't ordered her out of the apartment, but the fact that he had still ate at him after all these years.

He'd gone to the theater to apologize, but Nicole wasn't there, either. No one would tell him where she was. Jake's belligerent demand, "Okay, where is she?" had not impressed or intimidated Adam Chambers in the slightest.

"Who?" Adam had responded with bland unconcern.

"You know damn well who. Nicole. Where is she? She should be here for rehearsal."

"She called in sick. She had a doctor's appointment."

Chilled panic knifed through him at Adam's words. He was too late! "What time was her appointment?" Maybe he could stop her. "What's the doctor's name?"

"How should I know?" Adam had shrugged his shoulders.

"You know more than you're telling."

"Look, Jake," Adam dropped all pretense. "She doesn't want to see you. I don't know the whole story yet, but I do know that Nicole has been with this company since she was a fourteen-year-old apprentice on summer scholarship. She's gone through a lot in her life, and I won't let you or anyone else bother her." He drew himself to his full five-feet-ten-inch height and lifted his balding head. A steely look from his iron gray eyes underscored his point. "Accept that fact and leave before I call security."

Jake knew Adam too well to call his bluff. Then the bitter truth had cauterized his pain, and he'd faced reality. She hadn't given him a chance to talk to her, to change her mind. She hadn't wanted to work out a solution other than the fastest, easiest way. A void of emptiness had settled in a corner of his soul then. He had been a creator of life for a few short weeks, had only known of it for one day, then it was gone. So was Nicki.

That afternoon he signed a contract to be the opening act on a cross country tour hoping to escape the pain and all reminders of Nicole. The songs he wrote on that tour proved it hadn't worked, but they had been his ticket for a recording contract. His initial single, *Where Is She Now,* had made the record album possible, had made everything possible. Yet the dark corner remained.

Adam. He had still refused to talk to Jake seven months later when he'd asked why Nicole hadn't appeared with the company. He knew now. Nicole must have been nearly due by then. Jake muttered a curse as it hit him that he didn't even know Brianna's birth date.

He pushed the chair upright and reached for the telephone beside him. Without hesitation he punched the buttons in the familiar pattern and waited impatiently to see if Adam had changed his phone number.

Adam's voice came on the line, and Jake spoke with quiet authority. "Don't hang up, Adam. It's Jake Cameron. When is Brianna's birthday?"

Dead silence greeted this opening, then Adam asked, "How much do you know?"

"Too much—not enough," Jake bit out. "I've been to the studio and seen them both." He hesitated a fraction of a second before forcing himself to add, "And I've seen David." He couldn't stop himself from asking, "Are they lovers?"

"That's for Nicole to answer," Adam said. "And if you've seen her, why are you calling me?"

Jake didn't like exposing his vulnerability, but he knew that Adam wouldn't tell him anything if he didn't fill him in on the afternoon's events. Leaving out only the kisses they'd shared, he told him what had happened.

"So I blew it," Jake finished. "I saw David there, fitting in the way I didn't, and I blew it." He rubbed his hand across the back of his neck, trying to soothe the taut muscles. "So now what do I do? I know you're Nicole's friend, not mine, but I need to know more. Hell, I was sitting here and realized I don't even know when my own daughter was born. I know it had to be sometime in September or October, but . . ."

"September twenty-first," Adam said quietly.

Jake closed his eyes, savoring this morsel of information and its bitter aftertaste.

"Before I tell you any more, I want to ask you some questions of my own."

"Fair enough."

"How much did you care about Nicole before she left?"

"What kind of a question is that?" Jake demanded. "Of course I cared about her. I offered to marry her."

"Offered . . . I see." Adam's voice held a note of mockery. "Tell me. If she hadn't been pregnant would you have *offered?*"

Jake felt the guilt rock through him, leaving him without defense. He had been too involved with the good life he was living to think about marriage. He had declared that too many musicians' marriages failed. He didn't want that complication. He had been very pleased with himself, and he had taken Nicole for granted.

"I didn't think so," Adam interpreted Jake's stunned silence. "So why did you keep looking. Are you just stubborn, or what?"

"I didn't want to believe she'd gone through with it," Jake confessed. "And I was afraid she had. Either way, I had to know."

"All you cared about was whether or not she had the baby?" Adam probed.

Damn. Had that been all? For five years he'd wondered, but had his only concern been for a baby he didn't know—or for Nicki? Remembering the echoes of her voice in his dreams and her phantom laughter in the wind, he knew he'd avoided the truth long enough.

"I loved her, Adam."

Adam said nothing.

"Dammit, Adam, did you hear me?" Jake repeated in exasperation, "I said I loved her!"

"I heard you the first time," Adam finally said. "Now for the trick question. Could you love the woman she is now?"

"What do you mean?"

"I mean that Nicole isn't the idealistic, lighthearted girl-woman you had your affair with five years ago," Adam spoke bluntly. "She is a strong young woman who's gone through hell and succeeded in spite of it. And she did it by herself." Jake heard Adam expel a long breath before he continued. "Brianna nearly died three years ago, Jake. I don't know how much Nicole told you because she's never talked about it since, but she didn't leave the hospital for three days. I doubt if she ever got any sleep worth counting. David and I tried to get her to rest, but she wouldn't leave Brianna's room. The only reason she ate was because he forced her to. She must have dropped ten pounds in the next two weeks—and you know she couldn't spare five pounds, let alone ten."

Jake's knuckles clenched and whitened as Adam spoke. Nicole

had passed over Brianna's meningitis without dwelling on the trauma she'd faced.

"I never found out how much Brianna's hospital or doctor bills were. Nicole wouldn't tell me. I offered to sign a liability agreement to cover the bill if she couldn't manage it, but she made her own arrangements. The closest she came to letting me help was to loan her the money for the studio. She's paid it all back to me, Jake. I figure she still owes the hospital. But she's doing it herself. She's got guts. And if you think you can come along now and expect to find the same girl you knew five years ago . . . or treat her the same way—"

"Yeah. I understand," Jake agreed. He had to. He had seen the subtle changes that afternoon. Along with the shadows in her eyes had been purpose and confidence.

"I hope you do." Adam paused. "What else do you want to know?"

When Jake replaced the receiver a few minutes later, he knew that Adam, at least, was no longer working against him. He doubted if David would ever cooperate. Ruefully, he admitted that he wouldn't either, if the positions were reversed. It was obvious to him that David loved Nicole and wanted her as much as Jake.

Picking up the receiver once more, he called his business manager. "Pete, this is Jake. Listen, I want you to make reservations for the crew and me to stay in San Bernardino until we leave on tour. I have some personal business to take care of there until we leave, and I don't want to commute for rehearsals every day."

When Pete began to argue, Jake cut him short. "There's nothing I need to do in the next few weeks that can't be taken care of from there. If you have to juggle a few things, then juggle them."

"Hey, what's eating you? You'd think someone was threatening a paternity suit or something," Pete joked.

Jake's face tightened. "Who said anything about paternity suits? What the hell do you know about it?"

"My God!" Pete's voice rose with shock and dismay. "I was just kidding, but you're not, are you?" Jake could picture Pete's weathered face drawing into the mournful expression of doom Jake knew so well. "I'll get Don on the phone—"

Jake broke in at the mention of his lawyer's name. "Keep Don out of this. Look, I don't intend to give you my life history on the phone. No one's threatening to sue me for anything."

"But there's a woman mixed up in this, isn't there?" Pete declared. "I'm your manager, Jake. It's my business to know if some groupie is—"

"She's not a groupie," Jake interrupted, "If you must know, she's someone I was involved with five years ago." Before Pete could respond, he added, "And she's the mother of my daughter."

"What?" Pete exploded, "Don't go anywhere. I'll be right over!" The phone clicked and the connection was broken before Jake could protest.

Jake checked his watch. Ten past eight. It would take Pete twenty-five minutes to make the drive from his Burbank apartment. He returned to the entry hall for the bag and books he'd left earlier. In the bedroom he dropped the books onto the tailored charcoal gray spread before taking the bag into the large white-tiled bathroom beyond.

At the sink he dumped his purchases on the counter before reaching into the drawer for a pair of scissors. He didn't hesitate, but firmly grasped a section of the thick black beard and began cutting. Ten minutes later he toweled away the last traces of shaving cream and surveyed the result. What he saw was a mildly familiar stranger whose skin below prominent cheekbones gleamed whitely. The contrast with the deep tan above gave him an odd, two toned look. Long dimplelike creases that had been hidden by black growth were deeper than he remembered.

The dimples reminded him of the dimples he noticed when Brianna smiled. It was incredible that she could look so much like Nicole, yet be so definitely his. She had the same lithe grace and delicacy of her mother. Her eyes were his, though, large for her face and as clear blue as a mountain spring.

Nicole's eyes no longer reflected the clear green innocence he remembered. Haunted shadows added a depth of character, like the shadings of light and dark in a fine landscape painting. She gazed at the world with the maturity of experience and adversity. It made her face more beautiful than ever.

He quickly stripped his hair-littered clothes and stepped under the stinging spray of the shower. As the streaming water washed away the last traces of his shorn beard, he found himself comparing the Nicole of today with the one of five years ago.

More than her gaze had matured. Her then-budding body now bloomed with full womanhood. Had childbirth made so desirable an alteration, or had time? She still had the slender grace that attracted a man's interest, yet her hips had ripened and her breasts were fuller. Jake couldn't explain the change. He was sure her measurements would record the same, but something had altered to make her even more desirable than ever.

This afternoon she had climbed the stairs ahead of him and he had watched the gentle sway of firm hips so lovingly embraced by her tights. When he had held her against him, kissing her, he had wanted to mold those hips to him, to explore the subtle alteration in her form.

Her scent had altered slightly, too. It was muskier, yet it still reminded him of spring flowers and ocean breezes. Her mouth, too, tasted richer. The soft recesses held more mystery, and her velvet tongue took as much pleasure as it gave. She was a heady mixture of the known and the unknown. Her responses had been familiar and at the same time, new and exciting.

Jake cursed the physical response the thought of her created and adjusted the water to run cooler as he rinsed the soap from his torso.

Back in the bedroom, he stepped into black jogging pants before sitting on the edge of the bed and sorting through the books he'd left there: *Out of the Silence, The Deaf Child and His Family,* and *The Joy of Signing.* He chose one at random, then leaned back against the pillows to read until Pete arrived.

Four

Nicole poured milk onto Brianna's breakfast cereal and handed her a spoon just as the telephone rang. A small tense knot instantly formed in her middle. Common sense told her only Jake would call this early, and the knot tormenting her stomach tightened as she reached for the wall receiver. It annoyed her to see that her hand was not quite steady.

"I had no right to pass judgment last night, Nicki."

Nicole knew that it was as close as Jake would come to saying he was sorry. He didn't like being wrong. "Apology accepted," She said, and she heard Jake's expelled breath. He started to speak again, but she cut him off. "Wait a minute."

Silence hung suspended while she searched for a way to make her feelings clear. "Before we close the issue, you'd better understand one thing." She could picture Jake's expression. He didn't like conditions either.

"I have no intention of discussing or explaining my relationship with any of the men I know, David included." She hesitated, then plunged on. "Any relationships you had before or after ours is your business. We both know you were my first lover . . . but whether or not you were my last is my business. Since our physical relationship is finished, there is no need for us to expose or inspect private matters. Agreed?"

"Are you so sure our physical relationship is finished?" Jake asked. His voice feathered her nerve endings with their husky timbre. "I doubt if you've forgotten yesterday afternoon any more than I have."

Nicole shivered, clasping her free hand around her middle in an effort to combat the ripples of awareness his words unleashed. Her fitful sleep had been filled with vivid and even more erotic dreams than those of the night before. This time her hands had felt the textures of his skin against the sheets, and his dreamscent wove spells of pleasure promises that her dreams could not deliver. No matter how intensely her subconscious fantasies stirred her, they were a pale substitute for what Jake offered . . . and what Jake offered was a pale substitute for what she wanted.

She could imagine no worse heartbreak or disillusionment than a relationship based on duty and obligation. Her parents had remained married out of duty long after all affection had died. They stayed together because of their only daughter, their vows, and convenience. There had been no fights, no ugly scenes, no adulterous love affairs . . . and no life.

Nicole wanted life. She wanted laughter instead of distant amusement, passion instead of passive acceptance, and shared quiet rather than the isolated silence of two people who merely occupied the same house and bed. She preferred to live alone with Brianna than to live with a man who just thought of her as a satisfying bed partner.

When Nicole offered no argument, Jake pressed the point. "No matter how many lovers you may have had since you left me, Nicki, I still turn you on."

She closed her eyes as her memory immediately supplied the sensation of his callused fingertips brushing her lips. "I don't deny that." Nicole fought to remain cool and detached. She opened her eyes and tangled her fingers in the telephone cord. He'd been her only lover. The memory of his gentle teasing, exciting passion, and warmly knowing blue eyes had prevented her from forming deep relationships with any other man. She couldn't let him know that though. If he did, he would know the power he held over her, and she wouldn't stand a chance if he decided to use it.

He had the right to be acknowledged as Brianna's natural father, but that didn't—couldn't—include anything more than distant co-operation from her. "But it doesn't change my conditions. Either accept them or all bets are off."

Jake heard the edge in Nicole's voice and knew he would accept her terms for the time being. He had no intention of fading away just because he'd made a fool of himself last night. Neither did he intend to make it easy. He wanted Nicole as aware of him as he was of her.

His talk with Adam made him realize how little he really knew of the woman who'd borne his child. He wanted her off guard while he discovered exactly why she held his mind and senses more than any other woman he'd known before or since. He had as much to learn about her as he did Brianna. So he would accept her terms . . . for now. David had been patient; he would be, too.

"We still have things to work out," he said. "Are you free for lunch?"

She agreed to meet him at eleven, and he relaxed for the first time since awakening from a short and restless night. By the time he had calmed Pete down the night before, and they set up a workable transfer of locations and schedules, it had been well after one in the morning. His performances generally kept him up far later, but he seldom met the sunrise as he had this morning.

His face itched, and he ran his palm over his unfamiliar morning stubble. He'd forgotten the itch. He hadn't forgotten mornings when

Nicole had watched him shave. She loved to tease him about the faces he made . . . and imitated him in the mirror until they both laughed and he had to stop shaving so he wouldn't cut himself. Then she would wipe away tiny traces of lather, kissing each spot until they stopped laughing and started loving. It was one of the reasons he's grown the beard. Shaving brought him too many memories.

"Right on time—" Nicole announced when she opened the door at exactly eleven. She broke off with a shocked gasp when she saw Jake's cleanly shaven jaw. Pain shafted through her as she looked at the man she remembered and knew best. A tiny, half-dried cut marred the tip of his chin, and Nicole caught her breath. A riot of short-circuited memories and emotions charged through her until she felt fragmented. Heat welled up as she remembered the salt-soap taste of Jake's skin when she kissed his freshly shaved face. She remembered, too, the slightly rough texture and the faint mint and musk scent that went with his flavor. *Oh, God.*

The firm lines of his sculptured mouth twitched before easing into his slow smile. "Surprised?" Jake's smile widened into a smug grin and he closed Nicole's gaping mouth with a gentle hand before answering his own question. "I guess so."

Nicole forced herself to step back and let him enter. "You didn't have to do that," she blurted. She needed to pull herself together.

"You like letting your mouth hang open?"

"I mean your beard. You didn't have—"

Jake's teasing expression vanished. "Yes, I did."

Nicole thought of the image that had become as well known as the popular music he wrote and sang. The pirate look the beard gave him added an illusion of fantasy when he sang a love song. That romantic rogue image always made his posters sell out within hours of release.

"But what will your fans think?"

"They'll think whatever they want," he retorted abruptly. His voice softened, and his eyes revealed a glimpse of vulnerable uncertainty. "I'm more worried about Brianna's reaction than theirs. Where is she?"

"In the bedroom putting on her shoes."

They turned toward the short hall just as Brianna walked into the living room. Brianna wore her favorite dress, a pale blue gingham with tiny white daisies circling the round neck and finishing the short angel sleeves that left most of her chubby arms bare. The short ruffled skirt had more of the fresh white daisies and accented her matching blue tights. White barrettes pulled her shining dark curls back from her freshly scrubbed face. In each ear were fitted small flesh-colored disks held in place by earpieces like those found on eyeglasses.

Nicole saw Jake clench his fists nervously, then relax them before he kneeled down to Brianna's level. The happy pride at having buckled her shoes without help faded to curiosity when she saw Jake. Nicole moved quickly to intercede and she spoke aloud for Jake's benefit more than Brianna's as she signed, "It's Daddy, Brianna. He shaved his beard so you could see his lips better."

Brianna studied him skeptically. Jake reached into the pocket of his cotton knit shirt and brought out the bright yellow butterscotch candy wrapper from the day before. Brianna's eyes lit with recognition and she laughed. She looked at Nicole and signed quickly.

"She says your face looks funny," Nicole interpreted with a nervous laugh.

Jake grinned, running his hand over his naked jaw. "She's right."

Nicole had to look away from the cocky delight that made her heart race. He might be vulnerable where Brianna's approval was concerned, but his natural confidence always took over when he made even the slightest progress. Few things daunted him, and nothing did for long. It made his uncertainty when facing Brianna all the more touching. It also made it harder to keep her resolution to remain distant.

Shyly, Brianna approached Jake to touch the pale skin below his tan. She moved her fingers to the firm lips, then smiled.

Jake smiled too, then said, "That's a pretty dress."

Brianna's smile deepened, displaying her dimples, and she lifted the hem so he could inspect the row of daisies along its edge. She put her forefinger and thumb together, then touched them on each side of her small rounded nose.

"That's the sign for flower," Nicole explained.

Carefully, Jake copied Brianna's example. "Flower."

"What kind of flower, Brianna?" Nicole asked. She knew Brianna liked the daisy trimmed dress because of the silly word game they played with it.

Mischief spilled into Brianna's expression and she giggled as the two of them signed together, *"A days-E."*

"That's a sign pun. We used the sign for day and put an E after it."

Jake smiled. "Is there a real sign for daisy?"

"Oh, yes. It's actually the same sign as flower, but with a D instead of an 'F.'" Nicole kept her voice light, but the strain of seeing the Jake she had lived with and loved so often made her efforts at everyday conversation seem brittle and inane. The afternoon promised to be longer and more of a strain than she'd ever imagined. The only way to end it was to begin. "Shall we go?"

Nicole signed again, asking Brianna if she was ready to leave. Brianna nodded and reached for her mother's hand, then hesitated a fraction of a second before grasping Jake's with the other.

Jake's heart lurched and he marvelled at how right the tiny hand felt in his. He cleared his throat, but his voice still betrayed him, "Let's go."

Once down at street level, Jake led Nicole and Brianna to a modest four-door sedan. He'd bought it the previous year because it was inconspicuous and practical for daily living in an area as accident prone as the Los Angeles basin. He'd driven it today for similar reasons. He didn't want to attract any more attention than necessary to the fact that he was frequenting Nicole's studio.

The last thing they needed was some ambitious reporter following them with an eye for selling half-truths to the tabloids. He'd made a point of being available to the media often enough to keep them from hounding him, but he didn't want to jinx the fragile truce he and Nicole had formed by exposing her to the glare of sensational hype. He opened the back door and helped Brianna into the child's booster seat he'd bought on the way to the studio. He settled Brianna into the seat, adjusting the various safety straps with ease.

"You did that like a pro," Nicole commented when he straightened and shut the door.

Jake grinned, pleased with himself. "The saleswoman was very helpful. Not bad for just one lesson, was it?"

Nicole waited until Jake had negotiated the traffic to the freeway on-ramp and merged with the fast-paced cars in the center lane before asking where they were going.

"To Redlands," Jake answered. He glanced sideways at her, then back at the road. "Nicki, I have a concert tour in England right after Thanksgiving that's been set for over a year. I'll be back the day before Christmas, but I'd like to spend as much time with Brianna as I can before I leave."

Nicole started to protest, and he realized she was afraid he wanted to take Brianna home with him.

He spoke quickly, before she could say more. "I know you're rehearsing your Christmas ballet, and I need to rehearse some new work with the band, so neither of us has much time to spare. But I think I've come up with a plan that will help us both."

He flexed his hands nervously on the steering wheel. He knew Nicole saw the gesture and recognized his tension. He stared straight ahead at the traffic as he drove, but he was driving more on instinct than conscious observation.

"My manager found a rehearsal studio we can use locally, and I've taken a room at the Hilton. I can rehearse in the mornings, then spend time with Brianna while you teach class and handle your own rehearsals." He flicked on the turn signal and changed lanes, working toward the off-ramp. "I want to make the most of the next couple of weeks, Nicki. I want Christmas morning with Brianna . . . and not as a stranger."

Jake heard the proud appeal in his tone. He hated having to ask for permission to see his own daughter, though he didn't intend to take no for an answer. He wanted Nicole to agree, not make him insist. The arrangement would make the hectic preparation for the Christmas ballet far easier for her. Surely she could see that.

He waited until he pulled into a small parking lot a few blocks from the off-ramp before turning to see Nicole's reaction.

As he turned to face her, Nicole forced herself to smile, even though her thoughts warred with her emotions. "You know I'll let you have as much time with Brianna as possible."

He grinned, warmth lighting his eyes until they reminded her of the gentle waters of a Caribbean bay, and her heart skittered against her ribs.

"I thought you would. That's why I thought you and Brianna should meet the crew. We're having lunch with them." He turned off the ignition and leaned back with a satisfied air. "After all, Brianna will be seeing a lot of them from now on."

"Now?" Her voice seemed very far away, and she fought to gain control of herself. "What did you tell them?"

Jake took her suddenly clenched hand in his, smoothing it open and stroking the palm. "Everything."

Nicole's hand clenched again, but Jake relaxed her grip, finger by finger.

"You know they couldn't see Brianna and not put two and two together," he said quietly. He looked into her eyes and she saw the protective resolution in his gaze. "I didn't want you embarrassed by speculating questions or knowing looks."

Nicole couldn't look away from the sincerity in his eyes. Jake would never knowingly hurt her, nor would he let anyone else. Yet the idea of facing his friends and knowing they knew about her past made her feel exposed and vulnerable.

Jake's fingers traced a soothing pattern across her palm, circling the base of her thumb. The callused pads of his fingers sent a wave of awareness through her, and she pulled her hand free before he felt the tremors that would give her away. "I suppose people aren't all that shocked by children outside marriage anymore."

He grinned wryly and ran his hand over his freshly shaved jaw. "They were more shocked about my new look than hearing about you and Brianna. After all, none of them have ever seen me without my beard."

Nicole smiled weakly as she pictured their dismay.

Jake apparently took her smile as encouragement and he assured her, "Now that they know about the two of you and know that I'm not trying to hide the fact that Brianna is my daughter, they'll accept you for yourselves."

Nicole stared sightlessly at her hand which Jake had captured again. Few people knew the truth about Brianna. Most assumed she was a divorcee or a widow, and Nicole neither confirmed nor denied their assumptions. She had learned to concentrate on the present, not to dwell in the past. But her past was presently stroking her palm and claiming a part of her future.

Jake drew her eyes back to his with a gentle finger along her cheek. "They're good people, Nicki. You'll like them."

"I'm sure they are, Jake," she answered huskily. Then she gathered her courage along with her purse and suggested, "Shall we go? Now is as good a time as any."

A look of relief, and something else, crossed Jake's expression then was gone. "Before we go in, there's one more thing I have to take care of." He reached over, opening the glove compartment to pull out a manila envelope. "I have something for you."

Nicole tensed, suddenly wary as he handed it to her. "What's this?"

"Don't get mad. I felt I owed you and Brianna this."

She didn't want to take the envelope, knowing instinctively that the contents meant pain.

"Go on, open it."

Nicole felt clumsy, her hands awkward as they struggled to manipulate the simple brass clasp. She reached in, pulling out a thick sheaf of papers bearing the same hospital letterhead she had seen every month for three years. She unfolded it, ignoring the small booklet that fell onto her lap. Inside, she recognized the documentation of Brianna's medical bills. She lifted the page, and the next. Each one was stamped *PAID*. Her mind numbed, and she struggled to comprehend the full impact of the invoices in her hands.

She should thank him, but the words wouldn't come. Deep inside a small trembling began. She hadn't asked anyone to help her during or after the dark days of Bri's illness. She'd made her choices and paid her own way ever since, no matter how difficult. She should be overwhelmed with relief and gratitude, but some part of her burned with rage. She didn't want emotional indebtedness. Jake didn't owe her anything. Bri was her blessing, not her burden. "I can't accept this," she managed to say at last.

"Yes you can, and you will." Jake retorted. Nicole heard the stubborn note in his tone and recognized the steady glint in his gaze. "You've raised Brianna for four years." He nodded toward the booklet in her lap. "If you open that you'll find it's a trust account. The balance is the difference of what you've paid the hospital before I paid the balance this morning, plus four years' equivalent of child support. My lawyer is making arrangements for regular deposits into the account until she is eighteen." Jake took Nicole's hands firmly into his own. "I'm her father, Nicki. If you won't marry me, it's only right that I should share the financial responsibilities."

Nicole didn't have to check the bankbook to know his version of child support would be generous. The balance probably equalled more than her total income for the same period of time, but she didn't want to see it. For Brianna's sake she knew she would accept it, but each entry would be a ribbon of pain binding her to Jake, each number a lash reminding her that Bri was the only tie they shared.

The show must go on.

The traditional saying mocked her even as it reminded her of all the times she had forced herself to keep dancing, even when her feet bled and her body ached with exhaustion. The heart was just another organ, a part of her body. If she could perform when her feet hurt, she could live if her heart did. She looked at Jake, and forced herself to smile while she said, "Thank you."

Carefully, she picked up the bankbook and folded it inside the invoices again.

"Aren't you going to look at it?"

"I don't have to." Nicole put the envelope inside her purse, making a show of arranging it inside so she wouldn't have to look at Jake. "I know you want Brianna to have security. I'll be sure she uses the money wisely."

He reached for Nicole's hand. "Ready?"

Nicole smiled stiffly and nodded. Her conscious mind seemed to have shut itself off. She didn't know what to expect from Jake's friends and co-workers, but she knew her instinct for self-preservation would see her through.

Jake unlocked the door to the rehearsal hall and Nicole glanced around her as she entered. The room wasn't large, but the number of people filling it made it look even smaller than it was. A clutter of cables, amplifiers, microphones, and musical instruments gave it the look of an oversized storage closet. Against the far wall were two long tables on which were spread a variety of salads, sandwiches, and drinks. More than a dozen men and women lounged around the tables as they joked and laughed with each other.

Silence sliced through the chatter when the group saw Nicole and Brianna. Nicole instinctively took Brianna's hand as she faced them. She felt the warmth of a blush start creeping upward as they stared curiously, but she held her head up and gazed at them without flinching.

Jake broke the silence. "Everyone, this is Nicole." He laid a gentle hand on Brianna's dark head, "and this is Brianna."

A short spare man immediately stepped forward to take Nicole's hand. "I'm Pete Lassiter, Jake's manager."

Nicole's first impression was of a man in his fifties, but she wondered how accurate that guess was when she took his hand and returned his greeting. His bassetlike expression was rather deceptive, and on closer inspection, Nicole revised her estimate downward by a good ten years.

A striking redhead joined them and introduced herself as Pete's wife, Valerie. Nicole hoped her surprise wasn't too evident, since the vivacious woman appeared to be Pete's opposite in every way.

"I'm also Pete's secretary," Valerie added as they shook hands. "We keep it in the family."

Jake led them around the room, introducing them to everyone. Marty played backup guitar, Kevin handled bass and an occasional flute, and F.D.R. manned the keyboard. George, the drummer, was a big, rough looking man whose arms displayed a liberal selection of tattoos. He bent down to greet Brianna, and immediately charmed her when he held up the universal sign for *I love you*.

Nicole quickly lost track of who was who after that. Lighting assistants blended with the sound men in her mind, and she didn't know if the tall blonde took care of makeup and the short pudgy woman handled wardrobe, or if it was the other way around.

When she reached the table where lunch awaited, the tension of trying to appear at ease prevented Nicole from taking more than a token selection. One of the first lessons she'd learned in dancing was not to eat before a performance, and she knew better than to break that rule now. No opening night could compare to running the gauntlet of Jake's crew, no matter how friendly they seemed on the surface.

When Jake and Nicole headed back to the car an hour later, Brianna clutched a stack of cartoons that George had drawn to entertain her. She lifted one, a caricature of Jake playing a guitar, to show Nicole when a breeze caught the edge of the paper, tugging it from her grasp. Before either Nicole or Jake could stop her, she dashed after the paper and into the street.

"Brianna! Stop!" Jake shouted an automatic warning as he sprinted after her. The squeal of braking tires made Nicole look to the side. She cried out at the sight of the bright red sport car bearing down on them both. What seemed like an eternity of slow motion was really only a few seconds as Jake and Nicole raced to reach Brianna before she could be hit. The driver of the car made a heroic effort, swerving to avoid the small dark-haired child who'd darted into his path without warning.

Five

With a desperate lunge, Jake reached Brianna, grabbed her around the waist, and spun around just as the car brushed by, narrowly missing them both. Nicole caught up as Jake leaned heavily against a van parked by the curb; her face as white as the paper that started it all.

"Are you all right?"

"Yeah."

Jake wrapped his arms around both Nicole and Brianna, hugging them to him, as though trying to convince himself they were all truly safe. Nicole buried herself into the crook of his arm and held onto Brianna as tightly as he did. She could hear Jake's heart pounding under her ear, feel his ragged breath. Her breath was as quick as his and with each breath she smelled the mixed aromas of laundry soap, talcum, aftershave and Jake. She knew his shortened breath and racing heartbeat were the result of fear rather than the quick sprint he'd made.

He said nothing until his pulse slowed and his breathing had evened to normal. His voice, though, still held a rough edge. "I didn't think I'd get to her in time."

"Thank God you did."

Brianna squirmed beneath Jake's tight hold, and Nicole stepped back to look into her frightened face. Bri's blue eyes swam in tears that reflected her fear. With a whimper, she reached for her mother. Nicole held out her arms in answer, and Jake shifted Brianna to her.

"Are you folks okay?"

Nicole turned to find the driver of the car, his face blanched from the near-accident, hurrying toward them. As soon as he reached them he began to defend himself. "She just ran out in front of me! I swear I didn't see her until she was in the street." He peered anxiously at Brianna. "Is she hurt?"

"She's scared, but she's fine," Jake answered before Nicole could respond. "It wasn't your fault."

"Man, that scared the holy bejabbers out of me."

The poor man was as badly shaken as Nicole and Jake, and he mopped his sun-browned face with his arm. "Well, I guess if she's all right, I'd better go on." He turned back toward the small red car where it was parked against the opposite curb. Jake and Nicole watched him get in and drive much more slowly toward the intersection where he turned and was soon out of sight.

Nicole put Brianna down on the street. She took Bri firmly by the hand and led her back to the curb, then knelt to face her daughter. Her hands moved eloquently as she reminded Brianna of the rules for crossing streets. She didn't scold since the incident made its own vivid impression, and she knew further explanation wasn't necessary.

Jake stood silently watching, his nerve endings sparking from the adrenaline that still washed like tidal currents through his blood. When Nicole finished, he reached for Brianna's free hand as they turned and prepared to cross to the parking lot again. Its small size sent another ripple of aftershock through him, and he forced himself not to pick her up and carry her across the street. Together he and Nicole made a show of looking both ways before stepping down from the curb and walking across the pavement.

As Nicole secured Brianna into the car seat, Jake discovered that fear left an acid aftertaste that burnt his tongue. In the instant he'd grabbed Brianna and lunged forward he'd felt the fast hard brush of the car's fender. If he'd been a millisecond slower, she would have fallen under the wheels. A shiver of ice washed across his skin.

He'd shouted at her to stop, but she hadn't heard his warnings. He remembered dozens of times as a child when he'd been saved from accidents by a warning shout. Brianna didn't have that advantage. What other dangers lay in wait for a child caught in a silent world?

He'd been lulled into a false sense of normalcy by Brianna's shining face and winning ways. His lack of communication had seemed more like a language barrier instead of a handicap that made her vulnerable to actual danger. The bitter taste floated across his tongue again, and he knew he had to act, to protect Brianna from herself as well as others.

Jake remained deep in thought until Nicole finished adjusting Brianna's seatbelt and her own. Nicole looked at his tight face and saw his fear had changed into something else, and she spoke quickly.

"Jake, it could have happened to anyone. Children are always running into the street without thinking. Nothing happened. She's all right."

When he didn't respond, Nicole touched his hand. The flesh was cold and he held the steering wheel with a grip so tight his knuckles gleamed whitely from the pressure. "Hey, it's all right—"

"It's not all right!" he declared tersely. He swung around to confront Nicole with eyes that blazed blue fire. "She never heard me shout at her. She didn't hear the car. She needs to be someplace safe."

Nicole jerked her hand away from his arm, and her eyes widened in surprise when she realized what he would say next.

"Brianna should be in a special school where they can watch her. She shouldn't be out where she is in danger. She could have been killed!" Fine white lines bracketed his mouth and his lips thinned. "What if I hadn't gotten there in time? What if that guy had been driving just a little faster? We can't take chances like that. If she can't even hear a warning—" He bit off his words as he pounded the steering wheel decisively. "She's going into a school. I know you couldn't afford a private school, but I'll call around and find a place that will take her and make sure this sort of thing never happens again."

"Like hell you will," Nicole spoke quietly, but with a note of frozen fury. "What happened back there could have happened any time . . . and with any child. Brianna's hearing had nothing to do with her dashing out into the street." Nicole could feel her anger thawing, becoming heated as she pictured the life Jake proposed for Brianna. "No, she didn't hear your warning, but that doesn't mean she would have paid any attention to it if she had."

She sat stiffly, her voice brittle and sharp. "You won't 'call around' and find a school that will take her, because I won't have her sent away from me. Biological accident doesn't give you the right to shut her up away from the world like some vegetable that can't lead a normal life. She doesn't have multiple handicaps—she's deaf, plain and simple."

Nicole's eyes flashed with as much fire as Jake's had, and she shook a finger in his face. "Brianna is a bright, normal child who just happens to have a hearing impairment, and no one, not even the man who fathered her, is going to stick her behind fences and out of sight just because she behaved the way any normal four-year-old would!"

Jake's eyes narrowed, "I have every right to take care of Brianna. She is my daughter the same as yours. Just because you refused to tell me about her before doesn't mean you can cut me out of her life any more." His eyes glittered with steely determination as he threatened, "If I have to, I'll get a court order to give me custody of her. I owe it to her to—"

"Custody of her!" Nicole laughed in disbelief. "What makes you think a court would let you have custody of a child who doesn't know you and that you can't even talk to? There's more to being a parent than the physical act of procreation. You don't want to play father—you want to play God!"

Jake stared at Nicole for a long moment. Tension crackled in the air, and Nicole felt the slight lift in the hair along the base of her skull.

"It's not playing God to protect—"

"You can't wrap a child in cotton and pack them away from danger like china plates! Hearing children get hurt too, and all children learn from their experiences. The key, though, is that they have to be able to experience something." She turned back in her seat, folding her arms against herself. "Just take us home and leave Brianna's education and security to me."

A faint noise from the backseat made them both turn around. Her clear blue eyes filled with confusion and a different kind of fright than before, Brianna sat in her booster seat watching them. The electric tension filling the car made up for the fact that she couldn't hear their angry voices, and Jake and Nicole realized they had both forgotten Brianna was witness to their argument.

Nicole's anger turned from Jake to herself. How could she have forgotten how sensitive Brianna was to the undercurrents of her surroundings. She understood how Jake felt; she could think of too many instances when she had hesitated to let Brianna explore her world, afraid that something would harm her because of her impairment. She looked at Jake, seeing a self-reproach in his expression that matched hers.

"I'm sorry. I wouldn't take Brianna away from you," Jake spoke quietly. "I was just reacting to the situation. She scared me witless." A faint smile of apology lifted his lips. "As demonstrated by my idiotic behavior."

"I understand how you felt." Nicole met his eyes solemnly, then confessed, "After Bri's meningitis, I wanted to keep her with me all the time. I didn't even want other kids around her for fear she would catch their colds and flus. I wanted to build my own wall around her so she would be safe."

She smiled ruefully. "Then I caught a terrible cold . . . and Brianna caught it from me." She shrugged her shoulders. "That's when I faced the fact that I couldn't protect her from the world. Instead, I have to make her a part of it. I have to treat her like any other child if she is going to be normal."

"I still want to be part of that world, Nicole," Jake answered. "You're right that I can't communicate with her the way you can . . ." His voice had a ragged edge that made Nicole ashamed of the bluntness of her earlier words. "But I'll learn. I intend to be more than a biological factor."

Brianna fidgeted again and Jake smiled at her. "Okay, Little One, enough serious talk." He looked back at Nicole. "Truce?"

"Truce."

He started the car and pulled into the street. "What time will you be through, tonight?"

"Late, I'm afraid. I have a rehearsal scheduled after the last class and we probably won't be finished until midnight." Nicole saw the shadow of displeasure pass over his features, but Jake replied with forced lightness.

"Then I'll call you tomorrow morning."

Nicole hesitated, knowing she would be adding to his pique, but she had no choice. "I have a meeting with the head of the symphony tomorrow to work out our ticket arrangements. Then I have to go by the printers and proof the mailers. After that I have to check on the costume repairs. I don't think I'll finish until it's time for classes to start."

"Okay, I guess I understand." Jake nodded, his face relaxing. "I'll call you Tuesday, though, and we can work out a schedule then."

They parked in front of the studio and Jake helped Brianna out of her seat. After the angry scene in the car, he wasn't sure whether she would let him lift her out, but she did. Encouraged, yet knowing he was setting himself up for disappointment, he knelt down and opened his arms.

"Good-bye, sweetheart."

To his delight and surprise, Brianna accepted his invitation and gave him a shy hug. Her hair brushed his cheek and her chubby arms pulled him close. She smelled of talcum powder and no-tears shampoo. For the second time that day, Jake experienced a flood of unfamiliar emotion. He stood abruptly and turned toward the car. "I'll call you Tuesday," he said gruffly.

Nicole checked her watch as she slipped the last sheet of cookies into the oven. The aroma of cinnamon mingled with hot apple cider and baking cookies. At the table, Brianna carefully arranged candy decorations onto the cooled ones Nicole had already frosted. Beside her, round tin containers held layers of finished cookies Nicole intended to freeze until the cast party at the end of her Christmas Nutcracker performances. The doorbell rang and she wiped her hands on a small towel as she started for the door.

Jake struggled through the door, his arms fastened around an enormous stuffed, white plush hippopotamus dressed in a fuchsia-pink tutu. Round satin slippers adorned the short stubby legs, and a rhinestone tiara was anchored on the cartoon-like head. Catching sight of his absurd bundle, Brianna gave a squeal of delight, and Nicole burst out laughing.

"Is this some kind of a hint?" Nicole demanded.

"Should it be?" Jake laughed with her. "I saw this in a shop yesterday and I thought you'd both get a kick out of it."

He held the great white toy next to Nicole as though comparing them. "I don't think you have anything to worry about. There's at least two or three pounds leeway before you'll look like her."

Laughing, Jake ducked when Nicole made a mocking attempt to swat him with the towel she still held in her hands. A faint dust of flour filtered through the air when it missed his shoulder. Brianna watched their actions with sparkling eyes and she laughed aloud when Jake dodged her mother's attack. Jake pretended to hide behind Brianna for protection which made her giggle even harder. Nicole continued the charade by signing a demand that Jake stop hiding and apologize for insulting her.

Hanging his head, Jake knelt before her and surprised both Nicole and Brianna by signing, "I'm sorry."

"Jake! Where'd you learn that?" Nicole asked.

Jake raised his head and grinned with boyish pride. "From a book." He stood up and gave Brianna the comic hippo as he signed, "Yours."

Brianna, her face radiant with delight, immediately began inspecting the shiny pink slippers to see if they came off. Nicole watched Jake help Brianna with them, the two of them discovering each other while they explored the toy. Jake glanced up while Brianna untied the ribbons that held the slippers in place and caught Nicole's gaze. She swallowed hard at the joy lighting his face.

Then the light in his eyes altered, and Nicole felt the heat rise in her body. His melting magic worked without him even making the effort to draw her heart to him. Her fingers trembled with the desire to touch the clean silk of his hair, to taste the rough skin along his pale jaw, to bury her face against the crisp hair on his chest . . . *Stop it!* She pulled herself up short when she realized what Jake must surely see in her expression.

"I . . . have to check on the cookies." She excused herself before hurrying back into the kitchen.

Once there, she pulled out the finished tray and set it on the stove. Turmoil bubbled inside her, and she went through the motions of turning off the stove and clearing up her utensils while she tried to settle the churning desire that flowed through her veins.

Having him laugh and tease her so outrageously brought the past back too vividly. In those days they would have carried the mock battle into the bedroom where they both would have surrendered to the passion that flared whenever they touched, even in jest. Now she hid in the kitchen, willing away the taut bowstrings of awareness that vibrated with the knowledge of what it would be like to be Jake's lover again.

"Need any help?" Jake's low voice came unexpectedly from

behind her, and Nicole's hand jerked, nearly dropping the bowl she had just rinsed.

"Sorry. I didn't mean to startle you. Here, let me put that away for you."

He took the bowl from Nicole's nerveless fingers, loading it into the dishwasher. She stood by the sink, unable to move even when he came to stand behind her. His hands slid around to lock together at her waist, and he bent his head to nuzzle the back of her neck. "You smell as warm and inviting as the cookies," he murmured. "Do you taste as sweet?"

Rivers of liquid fire washed through her, and she luxuriated in the sensation of his lips teasing the narrow line behind her ear. He touched his tongue to her flesh, its hot moist texture trailing a path down to the base of her neck. She wanted to feel that damp roughness igniting the rest of her body, awakening those dancing pulsations she had tried to forget. She wanted to test the tender flesh at the edge of his collarbone, to see if it still excited her with its contrast to the hair-roughened skin of his chest. She wanted . . .

"Jake, don't." Nicole forced herself to turn from him, her body chilling when she moved away from the circle of his arms and the drugging pleasure of his mouth. "Bri might come in and . . . I have to clean up the kitchen and . . ."

"And the invitation in your eyes a few minutes ago wasn't meant to be an invitation," Jake finished for her.

Nicole flushed, but forced herself to face him. "No, it wasn't."

"I was afraid not," he muttered ruefully. He caressed her lower lip with his fingertip, then flashed a wicked grin. "But it was an attractive thought."

He picked up a spatula and began removing the cookies Nicole had left to cool earlier, shifting them to the table where the others waited for her to frost them. The action masked his frustration. He hadn't really meant to follow up on Nicole's obvious desire, but her fragrance caught him when he took the bowl, and he had to touch her. Touching, then kissing, were too familiar a set of actions for him to ignore.

Touching her. He wanted to do more than just touch her. He recognized the deep pull that made it impossible to ignore the net of emotions that held him, anymore than he could ignore his body's reactions. She was such a small woman, yet her grace held power, her softness overlaid firm strength, and her fine bone structure captured a classic vitality that intrigued him. She despised trading on her delicate appearance, and the fascinating melding of the fragile outer shell to the independent inner woman roused him as no other woman had.

"How soon is your next class?" He kept his voice light though the air quivered with the need for them to touch again.

"Not until eight. I have an assistant teacher who takes the Tuesday-Thursday beginner classes." Nicole's voice masked the raw nerves that screamed for her to turn back to him, to taste that small tender patch of flesh the way she wanted.

A giggle at the doorway made Nicole turn around, and the sight of Brianna standing there, the hippo's round slippers flopping on her narrow feet, melted the worst of her tension, and she chuckled with relief and amusement. Jake had turned, too, and his laughter held the same note of release.

"Why don't you stay and have dinner with us, Jake? We're just having soup and sandwiches, but you can help Bri finish the cookies while I get it ready."

Jake looked at her, his expression reflecting his gratitude for not making him ask. "Thanks, I'd like that."

He turned back to Brianna and pointed at the cookies. He didn't need to know formal sign language to make his point, and soon the two of them were working together, father and daughter.

After dinner Jake and Brianna helped Nicole finish cleaning the kitchen. A pang for what might have been again washed over Nicole as they worked side by side, rinsing dishes before loading them into the dishwasher. Jake became Brianna's pupil as she taught him the signs for dish, glass, dry, and the other utensils they handled.

Returning to the living room when the job was done, Brianna paraded her toys for Jake's inspection. Naming each one in sign, Jake learned the signs for doll, horse, car, and ball. When it looked like Brianna would move everything she owned into the living room, Nicole stopped the lesson. "Hey, there isn't room for all your toys in here. Besides, it's time for you to go to take your bath and get ready for bed."

Brianna didn't want to give up her spotlight any more than she wanted to go to bed. When she pointedly ignored her mother by turning her back and pretending not to see Nicole's instructions, Jake saw a stubborn determination he'd not seen before.

He remembered how he, too, had pretended he hadn't heard his parents tell him to do something he didn't want to do. Only his excuse had been that he hadn't heard them over the music he played. He'd tried to play one parent against the other, too, just as Brianna was doing now. She knew he was enjoying their sign language school as much as she was and thought he would let her get away with her small defiance. Brianna knew how to make her silent world work for her, and Jake had to fight to keep from laughing at his daughter's show of independence.

Now he knew how easily his parents had seen through his ploys. He turned Brianna around to face her mother again, and pointed. Reluctantly, Brianna went into the bathroom where Nicole bathed her, then sent her in to put on her nightclothes.

Nicole walked back to the living room, her pulse jumping when she saw Jake sitting on her couch, his hand rhythmically fingering the velvet pillow under his hand. He looked so right sitting there waiting for her while their daughter got ready for bed. The sweet confectionery scent of cookies still warmed the room and added to the homey tableau of family.

When he smiled, her nerves danced with involuntary reminders of other homey activities like snuggling . . . and lovemaking. Once Brianna was in bed they would be alone again, and Nicole felt the fine tensing of tender places that craved his touch.

She'd learned long ago that she couldn't have everything she wanted, and sat on the couch opposite Jake. She needed to set a less cozy atmosphere. She needed to find a topic that kept conversation light and the air mellow instead of crackling with invisible desires. She gave him her best *be-nice-to-the-rich-patron* smile.

"So tell me. What's it like to be rich and famous, Jake?"

Jake shot her a guarded look, and she knew her sudden choice of conversational topics didn't fool him. Still, he went along with it by commenting, "It has its advantages. I have all the material things I could ever want, and I've seen most of the major cities in the world. It's even let me enjoy some of the things money isn't supposed to supply."

"Oh?" Nicole didn't trust herself to say more, but she remembered too well the proverbs regarding money and love.

"A couple of years ago—right after my *Sad Days, Lonesome Nights* album was released, a woman from a little town in Colorado wrote me to say the title song was a favorite of her son's. He suffered from a blood disease and had to spend several days at a time in the hospital each month for testing and treatment. Anyway, she said Gary always took that tape with him to listen to after the family went home each night. It made him feel like he wasn't the only one who had problems.

"I flew to Colorado the next day and met him. What a terrific kid." Jake cleared his throat, and Nicole saw the self-conscious way he glanced away before he said, "If I hadn't been famous, I would never have known about him. If I hadn't been rich I couldn't have."

"What happened to him?"

"He's in remission now. I see him a couple of times a year. Whenever I do a concert in the area I send him tickets for his family and friends." Jake chuckled. "He says his popularity at school goes up every time the kids hear I'm going to be in town." His face sobered and took on a sardonic twist. "Of course that's one of the less pleasant parts of being famous."

"You can't really blame them for wanting free concert tickets," Nicole chided him. "Who wouldn't? At least Gary seems to recognize the difference between his real friends and the ones looking for a free ride."

Jake nodded. "That he does. He sees more than I did during the first years." He shook his head ruefully. "I threw parties for people I didn't know, went to parties given by people I didn't like . . . and bought six cars."

"Six cars?" Nicole laughed. "Whatever for?"

"Just because I could, I guess. I never did figure that out. Fortunately I came to my senses and hired Pete. Now I only go to occasional award banquets and small parties with people I like."

" 'Jake Cameron, the recluse of show business,' " Nicole quoted from a major tabloid. "Still, I seem to recall seeing several pictures of you with incredibly gorgeous women. Surely that wasn't all gossip hype." Nicole tried to keep the bantering tone in her voice and her expression lightly teasing, but she averted her face as she waited for his response.

The sight of those women smiling into his eyes and clinging to his arm had always caused pain to shaft through her. That first week she had told Jake that their lives apart were not each other's business. She meant it, but she still hoped the tabloid exposes were as false as so many others had proved to be.

"No," he confessed. "It wasn't all hype. Of course, some of it was wishful thinking on the part of the reporters," Jake added dryly. "I doubt if any man has that much stamina."

Nicole's heart constricted and she cursed herself for bringing the subject into the conversation. She tried for a quick comeback, something witty and worldly wise. Failing that, she simply smiled with what she hoped was amused understanding.

Brianna came in, her hair slightly damp from her bath, and Nicole helped her button her nightgown. Jake helped Nicole tuck her in before they finally turned out the light and left the room.

"She's so fantastic, Nicole," Jake said when they sat on the couch. "I wish . . ." he began, then shook his head, "Never mind. We can't go back."

"I'm sorry, Jake," Nicole replied to his unfinished thought. "I wish things could have been different, too. But we can't change the facts." She sighed. "I did what I thought was right." She looked at him, her expression sober. "I still think it was right."

"That depends on what part you're talking about. I agree you were right to keep Bri and to care for her the way you have. I disagree with the fact that you let me think you refused to have her and prevented me from being a part of her life."

The past again. It raised a wall between them anytime they tried to talk. It didn't surprise her. It did sadden her that breaking a trust left such festering, unhealing scars. "That's much easier to say now than it was then," Nicole retorted. "We've both changed a lot since then. Now it might be wrong—five years ago it was right."

"How can you say that? We're basically still the same people we were."

"No, we're not, Jake. At least I'm not." Nicole looked at him and her voice reflected the confidence gained through years of experience and questioning. "I see changes in you, too, even if you won't admit them. Maybe you don't see them yourself."

A tender smile softened her criticism, "You just told me how you learned to be wary of instant fame and money-based 'friendships.' Whether you like it or not, that kind of thing has changed the way you relate to people." She reached out to touch his arm in an unconscious gesture of supplication.

"If, when you walked into my studio night before last," she challenged, "I had welcomed you with open arms, said I'd marry you, and closed the studio. What would you have thought?"

Jake stared at her for a moment before answering slowly, "I'd have thought you might have realized that you cared about what we once had."

Nicole felt her heart constrict, but knew she'd hurt him too much for it to be true. "No, you wouldn't," Nicole said. "You would have considered me as selfishly ambitious as you thought I was when I walked out five years ago." Her smile became ironic as she continued, "And now that I've brought it up, you'll find yourself wondering if my refusal to marry you is some devious plan to take you off guard. It's human nature."

Jake made no answer, but his sober expression told her she'd struck a nerve.

"Cheer up," Nicole comforted him, "I don't have any intention of marrying you."

Six

"That last movement was too sloppy, Kristen," Nicole called. She caught the edge of impatience in her voice and made an effort to soften her criticism. "That turn has to be crisp. Hold your head arched like this."

She demonstrated the movement, the turn sharp, her body graceful. ". . . and watch your elbow. Don't let it get too angular. Start again from the same place."

Rehearsals had been longer and more closely scheduled during the last week, and Nicole felt the strain. This one should have finished an hour ago, but everyone seemed to be having an off night. "Hang in there, people. One more run through and I promise I'll let you go." She encouraged them with a tired smile. "I know you're all beat, but try to put some *ummmph* into it."

The prickling at the back of her neck told her Jake stood on the balcony of her apartment watching them work. He had arrived midafternoon to stay with Bri so that Maggie could devote her time to the studio phone and ticket sales.

Nicole turned, giving Jake a small smile of acknowledgment as she set up the tape recording again. "Okay, gang, this is it. Pretend your mother is watching . . . or better yet, a scout for the New York City Ballet."

Jake watched as Nicole led her class through the sequence for the tenth time. The grueling demands she made on the class seemed almost too much to ask, yet he knew she'd done most of the repetitions with them. And before that she'd danced with them through a different variation. She'd been alternately dancing and monitoring, correcting, and encouraging three separate groups of dancers since five that evening.

Her endurance made him sweat. She leapt, landed, and swirled—a snowflake tossed by the wind—and he knew the sudden dampness that sheened his body came from looking at her more than at what she did. He shouldn't torture himself by standing on the balcony drinking in the sight of her when she was preoccupied with her classes and rehearsals. He shouldn't, but he couldn't seem to help himself.

The burgundy leotard she wore hid none of the pulse points it covered, and her rapid breathing pulled his gaze to the sweat-darkened patch between her breasts. Her skin had flushed pink with the exertion, making it glow with vitality. He gripped the balcony rail to combat the too familiar surge of heat that rose every time he looked at her.

Nicole touched so many lives through her studio. From one moment to the next she encouraged a disillusioned student, demanded punctuality from a delivery company, or soothed an harassed mother who claimed not to have time for chauffeuring her child to rehearsals in addition to classes as the production demanded more and more time from everyone.

He'd never spent much time around her world when she'd lived with him. He'd usually expected her to meet him at the clubs and wait for him at the tables in the audience until the final set finished and he was ready to go home. If her performance kept her later than him, he went to the apartment until she got home. He only joined her at the cast parties or dropped her off at the studio.

God, he'd been a selfish bastard. No wonder she hadn't wanted to marry him. If he'd ever taken the time, he would have discovered she was a hell of a woman, not just a hell of a lover.

Nicole punched the start button, clapping to underscore the beat. "One, two, three, four . . . one, two— Much better." The dancers turned, leapt, and seemed to float across the floor, forcing their tired bodies to appear light and energetic.

Nicole knew just how hard they worked and that she could ask no more of them tonight. The music ended, and she applauded their effort.

"Okay, get out of here." She waved them toward the door. "But don't forget, same time, same place, tomorrow. Lori and Mark, I need you at four. Better bring your dinner."

Nicole locked up and made her way wearily up the stairs. Jake stood at the top, waiting for her. A current of warmth eddied around the vicinity of her heart. She could almost convince herself that he looked forward to the few minutes they spent together at the end of the day as much as she did.

"They looked good that last time," he commented.

"Didn't they?" Nicole felt a little of her exhaustion lift. "They couldn't have done it again, though."

"I don't think you could have, either." His eyes reflected a note of respect and he smiled wryly. "You must have demonstrated every move three times for every time they tried it."

"Haven't you ever heard the axiom, actions speak louder than words?"

He chuckled, and Nicole savored the delicious sweep of warmth the sound created as it rumbled around her. This past week she had become dangerously familiar with Jake's presence again. True to his plan, he arrived each afternoon before her first class. Jake took Bri to the park until dark or entertained her in the apartment. In the evening he fixed Bri's dinner and even tucked her into bed. Nicole felt his proximity as he sat in her living room while she taught her classes and ran rehearsals.

Maggie had done the same services for her before Jake did, yet Nicole had seldom been conscious of Bri's laughter beyond the French doors, or of the quiet when she slept. Jake's warmth filtered down to her, touching her, whether she adjusted a student's turnout or demonstrated a combination of steps. No matter how fierce her concentration, some small pocket of her being knew where he was and what he was doing every minute he was near.

She was conscious of him now. Tired as she was, tiny sparks of energy darted through her, and she moved away from him. She needed to tell him good night, to send him back to his hotel.

No.

She needed him to stay. She needed to bask in the cushion of warm belonging his closeness always gave her. Instead, she sat at the far end of the couch.

"You didn't eat anything tonight." Jake looked at Nicole, seeing the mark her increased schedule left on her body. The delicate look had become fragile, her face pale and her eyes shadowed. She worked off what little she had time to eat, and though he knew she didn't purposely avoid food, she often skipped meals.

"We had another minor crisis with the ticket booth just before you arrived, and then I got that call from the symphony that made me late in starting rehearsals." She looked up, clearly unwilling to move. "Now I'm not hungry anymore. Don't worry, I'll drink some milk in a few minutes before I go to bed . . . and I'll make sure I get a good breakfast in the morning."

"Too late. I saw you weren't going to get dinner, so when I took Bri out I picked up something for you."

"I don't like to eat just before bed—"

"Well, you're going to." He gently pulled her up from the couch and turned her toward the bathroom. "You'll sleep better if you take a warm shower to relax, then take a little time to eat."

Jake led her to the bathroom, not giving her the chance to protest. Once she'd closed the door and he heard the shower start, he went back to the kitchen and loaded a tray with the late snack he had ready.

When Nicole came out of the bathroom a few minutes later, he set the tray on the coffee table, then sat beside her on the couch.

"I made sure it wouldn't be too heavy, but you need more than milk." The tray held two mugs of hot apple cider and a plate with cubes of cheese and slices of fruit. Another plate held a small assortment of muffins.

Nicole's stomach rumbled, and she gave a low laugh. "I guess I need more than milk after all." She looked at Jake, her eyes soft with gratitude. "Thank you."

Jake couldn't look away from the warmth of Nicole's eyes. Their green depths jolted his body into awareness as no others ever had, and he struggled to keep from pulling her into his arms. She needed food, not passion. He couldn't drain her of what little reserves she had left simply because her eyes were the color of deep tropical lagoons.

He'd watched her every day this week, and her neverending schedule made his road tours look like afternoon picnics in the park. He'd seen the unguarded moments when the adrenaline quit taking up the slack and her energy drained away, leaving her a shell. Then someone or something would demand her time, and she pulled strength from some hidden well within her and started all over. It left him amazed every time he saw it happen.

Added to this, she arose with Brianna every morning. They had breakfast together before Nicole took her to the special preschool program for the deaf, then did mother-and-daughter things together before the classes and rehearsals began again after lunch. While Brianna attended her preschool, Nicole cleaned, shopped, and attended to the business end of her studio.

He'd never thought about Nicole's strength when they were lovers. He had sensed it. In fact, he knew now that her strength had been one of the factors that had fascinated him. Yet he'd not looked beyond the passion she fired with the turn of her head or the laughter in her eyes. When they loved, she had given everything. Yet she had never shown him the deeper core of steel that made her what she was. What would it be like to love her now that her steel had been tempered by time and experience?

Heat formed low in his body, and he tried to ignore the heavy, pulsing demand it made when he brushed Nicole's leg with his. He shifted away before he could act on the impulse to lunge at her like some hormone-engorged teenager. He searched his mind for something to say, but drew a blank. He decided with disgust that hormones left no intelligence in their wake.

Nicole offered him his mug before selecting a slice of apple from the tray. "Protein, fruit, and carbohydrates. Have you been studying nutrition the last couple of years, Jake?"

Nicole tried to keep her voice light, but she feared he would hear the wobble that threatened her control. His concern for her well-being touched her more than it should. He had done similar, thoughtful things for her in the past. Then why did she feel like crying because he fixed a simple meal for her? Her throat ached with tightly held emotion. She sipped the apple cider, then gasped when she realized the cider had been laced with rum.

"Whoa! Take it easy, Nicole." Jake caught the cup before she spilled the contents. "I meant to warn you about the rum. I thought it might help you sleep."

In catching the cup, Jake caught her hand as well, and Nicole knew her need to cry didn't come from Jake's thoughtfulness, but from the frustrated awareness that filled her every time he was near.

"Exhaustion is all I ever need to sleep," Nicole managed to choke out.

She saw the hunger that flared in Jake's eyes and heard the raw desire in his voice when he said, "You always slept deeply . . . when you finally got to sleep."

His gaze held hers, and the tension that had grown for days seemed to pulse around her, threatening to suffocate her with its close heat.

"Jake, don't—"

"Don't what?" His voice carried the same tightness she felt. "Don't remember the intimate things about you? I can't help it."

"Then don't talk about it." Nicole didn't want him to remember any more than she wanted to be reminded. As though she needed to be. His low voice stroked her skin as surely as his hands had in the past. A deep ache filled her breasts, their nipples painfully straining for the thrilling massage of his callus-roughened fingertips. His hands had played her body as surely as they did the strings of his guitar. They could never go back to that.

"Why shouldn't I? Do you think not talking about it will make it go away?"

Jake moved closer, his hand lifting to stroke Nicole's cheek, and her eyes closed as she tried to ignore the effects of his touch. When the faint residue of resin floated in the air she knew he'd been playing his guitar until Bri went to bed. The caress barely whispered past her face, but it electrified her senses. Her body heated, ready to receive his attention, despite the warnings of her practical mind. She fought the urge to turn her face into his hand, capturing its palm with her lips.

When he spoke again, his voice was low and gently commanding, "Look at me, Nicki."

She opened her eyes to find his face close to hers, and time hung in a balance. The past, the present, and the future all radiated from him as she waited for him to kiss her.

"What we're feeling has nothing to do with the past, you know." Jake whispered the words with fierce assurance, as though daring her to deny it. "You want me to make love to you just as much today as you ever did . . . not because of the memories, but just because you do." He gathered her closer, his hands sliding gently, yet possessively along her arms and back. "And I want to make love to you even more than I ever did before."

Nicole knew she should tell him he was wrong, that the tension that shimmered in the air when they were together was the result of awkwardness and guilt, but she couldn't. They both knew he was right, and she was too tired to fight her feelings any longer.

His lips finally touched hers, but only brushed the corner of her mouth. Before she could protest, they touched again, each kiss as light as a butterfly wing even though she felt them flow like lava through her veins.

"Kiss me back, Nicki," Jake whispered, his lips so close she could feel them move though they made no actual contact. His breath stirred warmly with his words, and Nicole knew how much warmer his mouth would be if she gave in to his persuasion.

Jake's hands continued their tantalizing massage, stroking her with a touch that made her skin quiver with awareness, and she couldn't resist leaning closer, letting the hard wall of his chest take some of the throbbing ache from her breasts. The thick terrycloth of her robe held no barrier to the heat that told her he burned as much as she. Her eyes closed, she felt the slightest graze of his fingertips as his hands left the cloth, skimming the slightly damp tendrils of hair at the base of her neck. He kneaded her flesh lightly as his lips teased her mouth, brushing them, but still avoiding the pressure they offered. "Kiss me the way you want to be kissed."

The invitation was more than Nicole could bear and, giving an inarticulate cry, she captured Jake's face between her hands. She pressed her open mouth hard against his, claiming what he had promised. Instantly, and with a groan that filled her mouth, he matched her urgency. He kissed her equally hard, making a mockery of the butterfly kisses that had only frustrated them both. Jake plundered her mouth with a passion that demanded satisfaction, and Nicole gave him all he demanded. He wasn't content with kissing her. His hands explored her with new purpose, gliding over her face, her shoulders, and arms, before seeking the softness of her breasts.

Nicole couldn't hold back the small whimper of pleasure that escaped when he cupped them at last, his palms grazing their tips before circling around and lifting their tender weight. Nor could she prevent the gasp of pleasure when he lowered his mouth to explore with his tongue what his hands had already discovered.

When Jake raised his head at last, Nicole could only gaze at him with eyes glazed with desire. His eyes burned with blue fire before he shut them, and he leaned his forehead against hers. His breath came in harsh gasps, and she could feel his heart racing in tempo with hers.

His voice held a rough edge when he finally spoke. "I knew I shouldn't have started this."

Nicole stiffened, his words stinging her conscience.

"Don't get me wrong, Nicki." He kissed her one more time, hungrily and hard, then pulled her back against his chest, cradling her gently. "I didn't intend to start this tonight, not when you're too tired to resist. I'm not prepared to protect you, and you're too worn out to be sure it's what you really want."

Nicole said nothing. Her pulse still raced, lurching unevenly when his breath stirred her hair, and she knew he felt the tremors that coursed through her body. Her mind told her he was right, and she should be grateful he had put a stop to things before they went any further. But her flesh didn't care about nobility; it wanted to be stroked, kissed, and satisfied as only Jake could satisfy.

Jake's low voice continued, "I know what I want. I've known it from the moment I saw you again. But when we make love—and make no mistake, we will—I don't want accusations that I took advantage of some past hold on you or excuses that you were too tired to know what you were doing. I want you fully awake and aware of everything we share."

A shudder passed through her as Nicole tried to pull herself together. Jake was right. If he hadn't called a halt to their caresses, if they had followed their desire to its natural conclusion, she would have made just those excuses and accusations. It disturbed her to admit that she would have latched onto a new lie when Jake had never been less than fully honest with her. He had never pretended to love her, though he'd made it plain he wanted her. It was she who hid behind lies rather than face the truth about herself. She wanted him whether he loved her or not.

She started to get up, but Jake held her firmly. "Just let me hold you for a little while longer, Nicki." His voice still betrayed an edge of tension held in check. "I've missed having you curled in my arms until we couldn't stay awake any longer."

Nicole leaned back into his arms. Her pulse still jumped irregularly, but less often, as she absorbed the warmth and security of Jake's familiar embrace. Slowly, the quivers of awareness gave way to the hazy contentment of knowing Jake missed their quiet times as much as their passion.

After several minutes, Jake whispered in her ear. "Nicki, come to the park with Bri and me tomorrow. I'm taking a break from rehearsals until we leave so we can clear up business and relax a little before the tour begins. Why don't you?"

Nicole felt a stab of disappointment that she had to decline. "I can't, Jake. The movers are taking the sets to the auditorium tomorrow, I need to be sure they—"

"Let someone else do it. You need a break." He brushed the back of her neck with his lips. "If all they need is supervision, Maggie could do it for you. Or David. You know he'd do it right." He nuzzled her again. "Say yes."

The idea appealed to her . . . and David had already offered to help supervise tomorrow. "I'll think about it."

"Say yes."

"I said I'll—"

"Say yes."

"Yes."

"Be ready by ten."

He wrapped his arms around her a little tighter, warming her like a cocoon and relaxing her more than she remembered in years. Her eyes weighed heavily against her cheeks, and she savored the contentment that washed like waves through her body. When she opened her eyes again, she was alone in her bed and Jake had gone.

* * *

Jake stared at the telephone, willing himself not to dial Nicole's number. The fact that he'd lain in bed staring at the ceiling for the four hours after leaving her untouched in her single bed didn't give him the right to wake her just to hear her voice. Knowing she wanted him as much as he wanted her made his attempts to sleep an exercise in futility.

Maybe when he was on his tour in England he would get some sleep again. He certainly got less and less the more time he spent close to Nicole. If he intended to make it on the tour in better than a vegetable state he needed to back away from cozy after-hour situations like tonight, not create them. Yet knowing he would spend the next day with Nicole made him feel like a kid on Christmas Eve.

He'd known better than to fan the heat that burned every time they allowed themselves to look beyond the flimsy wall of pretense they had erected in order to share Brianna. Yet they couldn't share Bri and not remember that they'd shared a bed. And therein lay the problem. They couldn't forget what it was like to share a bed, but the time wasn't right for them to try again.

Odd what life taught a person about timing. Every student of dance, music, or drama worked daily to master timing. It was crucial to the success of anything, but no one gave lessons in timing for relationships.

He remembered the night Nicole had watched a late-late movie on television. The heroine had been a child when she met the man who was her soulmate, but some quirk of time had allowed her to grow up out of sync. She had been able to catch up in age with the man until they could realize the love that would have been lost because of an accident of birth. Nicole had cried at the end because they were torn apart almost as soon as they had experienced the love that had made the miracle possible.

At the time he hadn't paid a lot of attention to why it had touched Nicole so deeply, but fragments of the story had surfaced ever since he had begun looking for her again. He and Nicole were not that different from the people in the old movie. They had met and responded before either of them was ready to do more than share a bed—

A bed again. Here he was trying to compare himself and Nicki to some great enduring love story and he couldn't keep his mind off of beds and heated bodies. He tried to be noble and explore the idea of a relationship based on something other than lust, and he ended up back in the bedroom.

Jake shifted uncomfortably. Just the word bed made his body ache. Probably because the word always formed with a mental picture of Nicole in one, her waist-long hair unbound and teasing him with glimpses of soft pale flesh between the long strands that acted as a curtain for her body.

If he closed his eyes he could feel the velvet texture of her tongue embracing his, dueling gently for the deep riches in the hidden recesses of his mouth. He could taste her sweet flavor even as he remembered the quick hard pucker of her nipples when he'd exchanged the heat of her mouth for the fullness of her breasts. The memory of her fragrance filled him with its rich promise and a fine sheen of perspiration broke across his body.

Damn.

Disgusted with his inability to control his thoughts, Jake sat up abruptly and swung his legs over the edge of the bed and headed for the bathroom. He hadn't taken this many cold showers since high school when his seventeen-year-old body had been unendingly aware of every female within a two-mile radius.

Sitting on the grass watching Jake push Brianna on the swings the next day, Nicole smiled contentedly. She had worked hard to appear unconstrained and natural when Jake picked them up that morning. To give him his due, Jake was working at it, too. In fact, after the first few minutes of strain, Nicole found that she didn't have to pretend to be enjoying herself.

Now, replete with fried chicken, biscuits, and coleslaw, she felt an overwhelming desire to stretch out and take a nap. Even as this thought floated across her mind, Nicole's eyes drooped and her head dropped slightly back to catch the gentle sunlight as it filtered through the trees. Thousands of people in the East battled gusting winds and blizzard storms in November, but here, in a California park, the sun shone brightly and she was ready to drift into sleep.

"Shall I fetch you a saucer of cream, M'Lady?"

Nicole didn't bother to open her eyes as she mumbled, "What do you mean?"

"I mean you look very smug and self-satisfied . . . like the cat who swallowed the canary."

A soft chuckle escaped before Nicole replied, "I feel that way. I was just thinking I ought to feel guilty sitting here when there are all those terrible storms in Chicago and New York . . . but I don't."

"You are an unfeeling and heartless wench."

Nicole lifted one eyelid lazily. "I know."

Jake sat on the grass beside her. Dapples of light made his dark hair gleam and caught the strong lines of his face. The stark contrast between his jaw and the rest of his face had blended since he'd shaved. Nicole felt the strong urge to reach out and stroke the firm skin. She closed her eyes, hoping to shut out the visual stimulus, but his voice acted like a drug on her senses.

"Brianna is trying to catch a squirrel."

After a few minutes he chuckled. "The squirrel isn't cooperating."

Another peaceful silence fell. Her eyes still closed, Nicole assumed Jake still watched Brianna play. The tantalizing touch of his fingers stroking her face opened her eyes in time to see his face descending, seconds before his mouth captured hers.

Seven

The kiss beguiled her with its gentle coaxing. Jake's lips were warm and firm against hers, taking her sweetness without demand. When the tip of his tongue teased the corner of her mouth, she turned toward it instinctively, searching for the taste that was Jake.

His arm encircled her, and he pressed his body closer. "I haven't given up, you know," he murmured. "I want you with me."

Bemused by the feathering kisses and teasing searching of his tongue, Nicole let his words go unchallenged for this one time. She didn't want to fight with him. She wanted to bask in his embrace while he lightly roused her senses. Her skin shivered with delight when his lips explored the softness of her neck.

"You've become a tantalizing woman, do you know that?" Jake

whispered. "The Nicki I knew before is still there, but she's only a small part of the exciting woman I met a few short weeks ago."

Nicole's eyes fluttered open as Jake's comment sifted through the purely sensual tide on which she had been floating.

"Motherhood suits you, Nicki," his voice went on softly. His persuasive explorations of her neck and face ceased, and he raised his head. His vibrant blue eyes looked steadily into hers. "So does the control you've taken with your life. You are so much stronger than I remember . . . and your strength is a magnet that pulls me to you as much as your vitality did before."

"Jake—"

Jake placed a gentle finger against her lips. "You don't have to answer, Nicole." He gave her a rueful smile. "I just wanted you to know that I see and recognize the changes in you. They're good ones." Once more he kissed her lightly, yet soberly.

"Have you recognized the changes in you?" Nicole asked him quietly.

"I'm beginning to," he admitted. "I've thought about what you said the other night at dinner. You're wrong about one thing, though."

"What's that?"

"I don't see you as a conniving woman out for what she can get from me." He smiled wryly. "If you were, you would have sold your story to the tabloids years ago."

"Oh, but don't you see?" Nicole pointed out. "The fact that you deduced that much means you considered my motives."

"But only after you challenged me to." Jake defended himself. "Before you stated your case, I never doubted your sincerity. It's one of the traits that is as much a part of you as the music you dance to."

"Thank you." Nicole accepted his compliment with pleasure. "What changes have you discovered in yourself?"

"I think I'm more mellow than I used to be."

Nicole tried unsuccessfully to hide her smile.

"Don't look at me like that," he protested mildly. "I mean I'm not in so much of a hurry any more. I enjoy taking time out to sit in the park and watch children play— Especially now that Brianna is one of them. I delegate more responsibility, instead of feeling that I'm the only one who could possibly do things right." Jake stared vacantly toward the swings where Brianna played. "I've accepted that I can't turn back time." He turned toward her with a teasing smile. "But tomorrow is another day."

Heat, then panic flashed through Nicole. His words held promise—and threatened the fragile facade of friendly distance she had convinced herself would protect her against her own feelings. Recovering her poise, she smiled in return. "That was the woman's line. The man walked into the fog never to be seen again."

Jake jerked as though she'd slapped him, then shot her a penetrating look. "I guess I had things turned around."

Too late, Nicole realized what she'd said . . . and that in their situation she had been the one to walk. "I didn't mean—"

"I know."

With the athletic grace so characteristic of him, Jake shifted his weight and stood, leaning down to offer his hand to Nicole. "Time for us to go. If you'll throw away the trash, I'll get Brianna into the car seat."

Nicole let him pull her to her feet and nodded in agreement. She hadn't intended to taunt him, but maybe it was better to keep their relationship distant. As she walked toward the car she wondered why she didn't feel more relieved that the wall between them remained intact.

Jake entered Nicole's busy studio lobby and approached the elderly woman who acted as receptionist at the registration counter. "Maggie, would you call Nicole and let her know I'm here to pick up Brianna?"

She looked up, setting aside the ledger where she had just entered payment for two little girls' lessons and reached for the telephone. "You takin' Bri out again today? I'd have thought you might want to take care of her upstairs since it looks like rain."

Since the night a week before when he'd told himself to back away from Nicole, Jake had made a point of having Maggie call up to the apartment and send Brianna downstairs rather than see Nicole alone. After classes were over he met her on the stairs and left with a quick good night. Unfortunately, he didn't seem to be sleeping any better for it.

"We won't be gone long, Maggie. I just need to—"

"Avoid Nicole again," Maggie finished with a sage look that told Jake she'd noticed the abrupt change in his routine.

Maggie Donnelly might be well into her eighties, but her mind was sharp as a tack and her wit equally pointed. Jake hadn't noticed her the first few days after finding Nicole, but the older woman had made her presence known several times since. Unruffled by Nicole's past, she had assessed him critically one afternoon while he waited for Brianna, then pronounced, "I can see why she chose you . . . but I'm darned if I can see why she let you get away." Then she'd shaken her head and gone back to making out bills. He wasn't sure, but he thought she'd muttered something about pride being a lonely bedfellow.

The main studio door opened, and Brianna ran over to him. He scooped her up and kissed her as she hugged his neck. He loved the sweet talcum and shampoo scent that swirled around her. He turned his face into the crook of her neck and blew air against it, making her giggle. Two short weeks had made him much more a part of her life than he'd thought possible in so little time.

Last week he'd let Brianna feel the side of his guitar while he stroked the cords. Her expression had filled with delight and she'd demanded that he do it again. Since then he'd put her to sleep at night by playing the guitar while her chubby fingers lay gently against the shiny finish.

The only thing missing was for her to trust him enough to try her voice around him. Her childish giggles filled him with joy and a terrible longing to know if her voice would sound as sweet. Still, he was learning to curb his impatience and enjoy Brianna's affection until he earned her trust.

Several hours later as he sat in Nicole's living room, Jake heard her students give the traditional applause that signaled the end of the last lessons for the day. He gathered the scattered score sheets with the arrangements he'd been trying to work on and stuffed them into his briefcase. Somehow he never got much done when he was close enough to hear Nicole's voice as she gave instructions to her class. With a final check on Brianna, he let himself out of the apartment and quickly went down the stairs before Nicole finished locking up.

Nicole spotted Jake as he reached the door to the lobby. She knew he'd been avoiding her, but she also knew they had to get past their feelings and start talking again.

"Jake, don't leave yet. I need to talk to you."

"What about?"

His voice held a wariness, and he halted several feet from her, as though he didn't want to get too close.

"I know you leave for your tour Friday, and since Thursday is Thanksgiving I wanted to be sure you knew you were invited to be with us." Nicole cursed the tight, prim way that sounded. "You can bring any of the crew who want to come, too."

"You have too much to do to fix a big meal like that. Let me take you out."

Nicole was startled by the fierce protectiveness in Jake's sharp retort.

"I'm not talking about just Brianna and me. It's a pretty big group. Maggie and the other residents of the apartment building who don't have family will be here. I just do the turkey, dressing, and gravy. The others each bring a side dish." Great, now she sounded like she didn't want to be alone with him. Did she? The past week had not lessened her awareness of Jake at all. If anything, her body seemed to have become an ultrasonic antenna, picking up his vibrations at all hours of the day or night.

Jake stared at her, as though assessing how much work the day really entailed. "Okay, of course I want to spend the day with the two of you. But I'll buy the turkeys—I'll take care of ordering the tables, too. How many will you need?"

"There'll be nine people from here, plus David, Adam and his wife, and my parents . . . that's sixteen with Brianna and me. So figure on four tables plus however many more you'll need for your crew."

Jake turned his head sharply. "Your parents will be here?" His expression held accusation and a flash of wariness. "Do they know about me?"

"Yes and no," Nicole hedged. She hadn't intended to let them meet without preparation, but neither had she meant to just drop the news to him with a slip of the tongue, either.

Jake raised one brow, his eyes piercing her with their suspicious gaze.

"They know you're Brianna's father. They just don't know that you know about her or that you'll be here Thursday."

"Don't you think it might be a good idea to let them know?" Jake's voice held a tight edge. "Or did you plan to let us bump into each other without warning?"

"Of course not. I'll be talking to my mother tomorrow. I intended to tell her then."

"When did you intend to tell me—when you introduced us?"

"Now." Nicole defended herself. "I just didn't intend to do it so badly."

The street sounds from below carried up the stairwell, accenting the stifled tension that filled the air.

"Let me get this straight. This little group includes your parents, who think I abandoned their pregnant daughter, David who would rather I'd never shown my face again, and Adam, who refused to let me contact you when I looked for you five years ago, and you didn't mean to handle it so badly." Jake shook his head, looked at the ceiling as though looking for inspiration, and then shrugged his shoulders. "It should be an interesting holiday. Are you sure you want me to come?"

"Yes, I do. But if you don't want to—"

"I'll be there . . . with bells on."

Nicole opened the door to her apartment, grateful that the next day would bring a break from the hectic pace of the past week. She would feast on turkey, visit with her neighbors, and relax. Relax? A raw laugh tore itself from her. *Jake's going to be here, fool. You won't relax.* After spending a platonic day with him in the presence of two dozen people she'd be strung tighter than the strings on his guitar.

The past few days, she had told herself her tension was because Jake and her parents were going to meet each other. But once she'd let them each know about the other, the greatest pressure had really been lifted. In fact, Jake had adopted an attitude of fatalistic humor that surprised her. His humor, in fact, had been one of the factors that added to, rather than eased, her tension.

When he made her laugh, he reminded her of the times they'd shared the same sense of humor. Laughing with him had always led to loving him, and since the night he'd told her they would make love again, she'd thought of very little else. Even her apartment had picked up his essence. She saw his presence in so many little things: a sheet of composition paper left in the trash, the trace of aftershave in the air, a discarded tie from the afternoon he'd returned from a business meeting. Yet, the distance he'd kept made her scorchingly aware of how good it had felt to kiss him, to have him hold her in his arms again.

She stepped inside, then stopped short when she saw the couch had been opened and Jake lay on the hide-a-bed watching the ten o'clock news. Her heart faltered, then raced, when she realized he wore a bathrobe, his long, lean and bare legs stretched the length of the bed. Something deep and elemental burst into life, spreading its warmth to her core and sending a shiver of familiar desire coursing through her veins.

The TV report about terrorist activities faded from her consciousness when Jake shifted and his robe slid open. The light from the television caught the gleam of his chest hair, and its rich darkness sent flames of remembrance to her fingertips and lips. She curled her fingers into her palm, trying to erase the rough texture from their pads, even as she tasted his salt flavor on her mouth.

Tonight?

Her pulse leapt in anticipation, though her mind rebelled at the idea that he had assumed she would easily agree to some calculated proof that they still wanted each other. When she spoke, she prayed her voice sounded less affected by the sight of him than she felt.

"You're liable to get arrested if you drive home dressed like that."

He turned his head, and she knew he'd known just how long she had stared at him before speaking. His eyes locked with hers, then his gaze focused on her mouth. Nervously, she licked her lips, then cursed herself for reacting in such a provocative way.

"I'm not driving home tonight." His calm statement sent another tremor through her before anger could stop it.

"I'm not going to make love with you tonight, Jake."

A slow grin curved upward, and he crossed his arms over his chest. "I know. I am here to babysit turkeys."

"Turkeys?"

"As in Thanksgiving, remember? I had the hotel get them ready, and I brought them over tonight. One of them is in the oven here and the other is at Maggie's."

"What does that have to do with you lying on my hide-a-bed in nothing but your bathrobe?"

"What makes you so sure I'm wearing only a bathrobe?" Jake challenged her with a grin. The glint in his expression told her that he'd meant her to think that. "Don't be too disappointed, Nicki, I'm wearing briefs, too. Fatherhood demands a few compromises." He adjusted the robe again, covering his sculptured muscles. "As to why I'm staying, tomorrow morning you are going to sleep late for a change. I'll take care of Bri when she wakes up, and you will finally get some of the rest you need."

Sleep in? With Jake in the next room? Nicole's blood surged with liquid flame at the thought of Jake so near during the night, and she doubted if she would sleep at all. Only a week earlier she had boasted the exhaustion was all she needed to put her to sleep. But she hadn't counted on him putting her to the test. Undershorts or no, she could envision his body too clearly to be unmoved by the thought of him lying there . . . in a bed large enough for two.

"What if I asked you to leave?"

"You know the answer to that."

"Just don't get any ideas in the middle of the night."

"That's generally when I'm the most inventive."

Nicole flushed. His double entendre held too much promise. She wouldn't win a war of wits with him tonight; the sight of him when she came in had robbed her of the few she had left.

"I just want your word that you won't try to get me into this bed with you."

"I can't do that." Before she could answer, he added, "But I will promise not to try tonight."

Escape was her only recourse. She turned and started briskly to her room. "Good night, Jake."

Jake watched her beat a hasty retreat into the bedroom, then leaned his head back against the pillow and let out a frustrated groan. He'd thought he could tease Nicole enough to keep her on the edge of awareness. He intended to continue until she admitted she wanted him as much as he wanted her. Unfortunately, he was more on edge than her.

Nothing but pure willpower and the knowledge that he would

lose more than he would gain had kept him from pulling her down onto the bed with him. The take-charge part of him challenged him to make love to her until she admitted that the platonic dance they had undertaken was nothing but a charade. His instinct told him to wait for her to come to him. He knew his instinct was right, but surely a little nudge now and then might speed things along. He punched his pillow and tried to relax. It was going to be a long night.

Jake's low voice coaxed Nicole softly. "Rise and shine, sleepyhead." Nicole stirred, aware of the morning's light on the other side of her closed lids. Still half asleep, she rolled over. When her body pressed against a firm wall of muscles and her lips captured a teasing kiss, she responded with delicious fervor, enjoying this dream more completely than any she'd had since Jake's return. He made a low animal sound of satisfaction, shifting her closer to him. Cold air touched her where the blankets no longer covered her, and she came awake with a start.

"I told you no funny business," she protested, pushing him away. The warmth of his mouth stayed even after he broke contact.

"Correction." His breath stirred against her vulnerable neck as he nibbled its nape. "I promised not to try to get you into bed in the living room. This one is in the bedroom."

"Brianna is in the next bed," she argued furiously. "What if she woke up?"

His lips created havoc with her self-control, and she tried to burrow deeper into the blankets to escape his marauding mouth.

"No, she's not," he informed her. "She's down the hall with Maggie."

"What?" Alarmed and disoriented, Nicole turned back, only to meet Jake's mouth again. The kiss held a promise that teased, and assured her she had nothing to worry about.

Nothing to worry about? She was as crazy as he was. Brianna wasn't here to act as a buffer, and she lay in bed with the one man she'd never been able to resist.

He raised his head, and the laughter reflected in his eyes sent her pulse into convulsions. "Maggie, the dear lady, knocked on the door early this morning to see if you needed any help. You," he punctuated his words with light cajoling kisses on her nose, forehead, and mouth, "were dead to the world, and Brianna was pestering me for breakfast. Your delightfully wise friend Maggie decided that she could cope better than I with Brianna—and she informed me in no uncertain terms that you needed more time in bed. So . . ." he teased the corner of Nicole's mouth with a playful finger. "Your wonderful, kind, thoughtful, and helpful friend Maggie is fixing Brianna's breakfast at her apartment." He slid his arms around her and pulled Nicole close, nuzzling her neck. "Isn't that nice?"

He chuckled when he drew back to see Nicole's expression. "Come on," he persuaded, "admit that it's nice."

A small smile twitched at the corner of her mouth, and Jake pounced on the chink in her armor. "Aha!" he declared gleefully, "a smile."

It was no use. How could she resist the man? "You win," she admitted. "It's nice." She buried herself under the blankets again and her voice drifted up, muffled by the covers, "Now, go away and let me sleep."

His rumble of laughter started deep in his chest before spilling out, filling her bedroom. "Then if you won't play with me, I guess I'll go have coffee with dear, sweet, thoughtful—and soon to be disillusioned—Maggie."

To her surprise, he slipped off the bed and left the room. Bed wasn't as interesting once he left. Nor could her body drift back into the cocoon of sleep now that it tingled with the imprint of Jake's body. Nicole threw back the covers in resignation and headed for the shower.

Jake didn't return to the apartment with Bri until Nicole had taken a leisurely bath, dressed, and settled onto the couch with her second cup of coffee. When he did, the twinkle in his eye told her more than words how much she had revealed in the half-sleeping response he'd stolen earlier.

When she could stand his smug silence no longer, Nicole returned her cup to the kitchen and began gathering the tablecloths to take downstairs.

"We'd better get the tables arranged before everyone starts showing up."

She started down the stairs, and Jake followed. In the ballroom, the furniture rental company had delivered several long tables which were stacked beside the wall, waiting to be unfolded and made ready for Nicole's guests.

"It looks a little like a medieval dining hall," Jake commented a half hour later.

Nicole and Jake stood back from the long tables they had just covered with a variety of white tablecloths. The tables formed a large "U" in the center of the ornate ballroom. Two long tables lined the narrow end wall by the double doors. Soon they would hold all the dishes of holiday foods contributed by the other members of the apartment house.

Voices drifted up from the stairwell, and someone's hearty laugh echoed off the walls just before several of Jake's crew came into sight.

"You're just in time," Jake greeted them. "Grab a chair and help me finish putting them around the table."

"Hey, nobody said anything about work," George complained. "Besides, I have something for Brianna. Where is she?"

"She'll be down in a few minutes. Maggie has been letting her help make punch while we set up the tables," Nicole answered.

"Shake a leg, George," Jake prodded him with a folding chair. "Bribing my daughter won't get you out of this. Besides, if you don't work, you don't eat."

George handed Nicole a thick drawing pad and a package of felt-tipped markers. "Hold these for me. When Jake starts something, he won't quit 'til it's done." With a grin and a shrug, he started pulling chairs from the stack by the wall and placing them around the table. Everyone else did the same. The last chair had just been arranged when Brianna and Maggie joined them.

George easily captivated Bri with the volumes of cartoons that flowed from his felt-tipped pens. Soon they sat in a corner, engrossed with drawing pictures of pilgrims and turkeys.

An hour later, the room reverberated with the chatter of people as the residents of the converted apartments mixed with Jake's crew. Nicole stood with Maggie and Mr. Rosen, the elderly man whose rooms were just beyond the main stairwell, when David tapped her on the shoulder.

She turned and greeted him with a hug. "You're late," She scolded him good-naturedly. "You were supposed to be here a half an hour ago to help set up the tables. It would have served you right if we started without you."

"You wouldn't dare. You can't do the *pas de deux* without me."

She laughed. "I knew there had to be some good reason why we waited. Brianna was asking about you earlier."

"I see her. I'll go let her know Uncle David is here, and you can go greet your parents. They were parking their car when I arrived."

It was a measure of her preoccupation that she'd forgotten her parents had yet to arrive. Most years she spent a good deal of her time double-checking to see that everything was as perfect as possible, knowing her mother would drop some comment about her duties as a hostess.

She watched David wind his way through the guests as he headed toward Brianna. Jake even acknowledged him when he passed, though the two men didn't talk long. She turned toward the stairs, reaching them just as her mother came into view.

"There you are, Nicole. Happy Thanksgiving, dear."

"Thank you, Mother. Hi, Dad. You're right on time, as usual."

Alice Michaels, at forty-two, looked sleekly casual in winter-white slacks and a sapphire blue sweater. As slender as Nicole, she didn't look old enough to have a four-year-old granddaughter.

"You know I've always said people who think it's fashionable to be late are rude, not stylish. It's the duty of a guest to be prompt."

"Yes, I know."

Nicole knew, too, that her parents came to the Thanksgiving dinners at the studio because they thought it was their duty as grandparents to acknowledge their granddaughter so people would know they hadn't ignored Brianna because of her handicap.

"We brought Brianna a present. Where is she?"

John Michaels looked as young and fit as his wife, but their shared look of youthful good health came from hours spent at separate fitness training centers and not a passion for the outdoors. A prominent orthopedic surgeon, John spent most of his time at the hospital, while Alice spent hers involved with charity.

Whatever her parents had shared in common when they married, it had long since been lost. The only thing they still shared was a firm belief in fulfilling their duty to the promises they had made in their marriage vows and in their obligation to Nicole and Brianna.

Nicole searched the room with a quick glance that told her Brianna and George still occupied the far corner of the room. "She's over there with one of Jake's friends."

"Oh. Then he came, after all."

"Of course, Mother." Nicole kept her voice as quiet and unemotional as she could. "He feels as responsible about his duties as you do."

"So much so that he ignored his child for four years?"

"So much so that he spent four years trying to find out if he was a father. I explained that on the phone Tuesday."

"I know what you told me, Nicole. But for four years you let us believe he had no inkling about her. I can't help but wonder if you're just trying to cover up for him now."

"If I were, then how did he find me?" Nicole felt her temper rising, but she held on, knowing that emotions had never impressed her parents and were certainly not the way to sway them now.

"She's right, Alice," Nicole's father agreed. "If she wouldn't contact him when Brianna was sick, why would she have done so now? He must have been the one to make the first move."

"I suppose so," Alice conceded. She turned back to Nicole. "You know you shouldn't have kept that kind of information from him. It was your duty to make him accept his responsibilities."

"So you've told me."

Jake spoke softly from behind her. "Won't you introduce me, Nicki?"

Eight

Jake had watched Nicole talking with the couple who could only be her parents for just a short time before he realized that the conversation had fired Nicole's normally even temper. Drifting closer, he'd heard enough to understand why. Her mother's cool voice irritated Jake, even though the woman's argument repeated the very charges he'd made to Nicole just a few weeks earlier.

Nicole made the introductions, and Jake found himself wondering at the undercurrent of distance between Alice and John. Oddly, it didn't seem like the distance created by friction, but it was something more like two strangers who shared the same name by accident rather than plan.

"I have to admit, I never expected to meet you," John said as the two men shook hands. "Nicole told us you hadn't any idea about Brianna."

"I didn't, really." Jake wondered how Nicole's father could speak so calmly. If their positions had been reversed, he doubted if he would be so civil. "I just had to know what had happened to Nicole."

"Now that you know, what do you intend to do about it?"

"Dad!"

Nicole's shocked gasp reminded Jake that she hadn't told her parents the details of their breakup. Much as the past rankled him, he didn't care to share their private lives with others any more than Nicole did. His reply held just the edge of a warning, even as he smiled.

"We'll do whatever Nicole and I decide is right for the three of us."

"John, we haven't given Brianna her present, yet."

Alice changed the subject with an air of innocence that Jake had to admire. She was obviously a woman who avoided the slightest hint of controversy or emotional response. After her comments to Nicole, he wouldn't call her a diplomat.

After Alice and John excused themselves to go find Brianna, Nicole turned to Jake with a rueful smile. "I'm sorry—"

"Don't apologize, Nicki. Things went better than I expected." He flashed his famous grin and tucked her hand into the crook of his arm. "Things always look better on a full stomach. Let's get this show on the road before I have to—literally. Remember, I have to catch a plane in the morning."

The remains of the turkey sat forlornly on the side table with emptied serving bowls and a single remaining piece of pumpkin pie. Nicole started to gather the bowls but was stopped by Pete's wife. "It's our turn now. You go sit down and we'll clean up."

In less time than Nicole would have believed possible, the ballroom had been cleared. The dishes were cleaned and stacked ready for their owners to take them home and the tables were pushed against the wall. The chairs now formed clusters as everyone visited in small groups.

"You know, I think it would be nice if Jake played us some after dinner music." Maggie's voice carried across the room to Nicole. "We need something to take our minds off our overloaded stomachs."

"I don't think—" Nicole began, but Jake interrupted.

"I don't mind. Let me get my guitar."

"Sing *Where Has She Gone,*" Mr. Rosen requested when Jake had slipped the broad guitar strap over his shoulder. "And *Leaves of Time.*"

Smiling broadly, Jake played the requests, singing them in his richly caressing voice. Each time a song ended, someone else called out a new one. There had been many songs over the years, and time melted into nothingness as each was sung with the simple accompaniment of the guitar. Kevin, Marty, and George occasionally joined in with harmonies, but it was Jake's haunting, teasing baritone that wove a spell of warm contentment.

Beside Brianna, Nicole's hands floated and swayed, singing the songs silently with him for Bri's benefit. The mirrors on the wall reflected her motions, and the crew, having never seen songs signed before, turned their attention from Jake's performance to hers. Jake's voice faded away as he ended a particularly gentle love song, and Nicole's hands seemed to carry the sound fading along with Jake's own voice.

"That was terrific!" George declared with enthusiasm.

"Yeah," Marty agreed. "We ought to take you with us. You could join the act."

"You should see her dance and sign at the same time," Maggie spoke up. "Do *The First Time Ever I Saw Your Face,* Dear." She turned to Jake with a gleam in her eye. "I've always loved to watch her do it. She really makes you feel the words."

Nicole looked down at the soft emerald chiffon dress and velvet heels she wore. "I'm really not dressed for dancing, Maggie."

Whenever she danced that song she felt the words in her very soul—and she knew it showed. It was a song that exactly described her own memories of the time before Brianna. She wasn't sure if she wanted Jake to witness that particular dance. Especially now that she knew her feelings hadn't changed.

"That didn't stop you last year," Maggie reminded her tartly. She nodded to Mr. Rosen. "Remember? She had on that straight skirt with the slit all the way up her leg."

Mr. Rosen grinned at the memory of the dress, and Maggie coaxed Nicole. "Just have Bri run up and get your ballet slippers. This year your dress doesn't look that much different than some of the chiffon dancing skirts you use; it just has a lining."

"Go ahead," David encouraged her from his seat on the other side of Brianna. Looking directly into her eyes he muttered, "Don't let Jake's being here stop you. If he hasn't figured it out by now, he never will."

Nicole realized he was right. Jake would watch the dance as he would any other performance. He wouldn't recognize it as the enactment of her true feelings.

David lowered the lights so that they highlighted the center of the oak floors, while Nicole took her place. She nodded to David and he started the record.

Roberta Flack's haunting voice flowed through the vast room as Nicole incorporated the beauty of sign language into the grace of the dance. The words captured the tenderness and wonder of Nicole's feelings. The melody lifted her beyond the limitations of earth and gravity as she floated on the waves of sound. By the time she signed the lyrics that spoke of lying with him, she was lost to the people around her. Her mind and body was with Jake, and the first time he had made love to her.

When the last notes faded, Nicole felt as though she was awakening from an erotic dream. Reality penetrated her consciousness slowly, her body unwilling to let go of the tender passion in exchange for prosaic conversation. Slightly disoriented from the transition, she looked to where Jake sat with Brianna on his lap. An oddly pained expression flickered between them for an instant, and Nicole knew that he had seen and understood how much the song's words represented the tender memory of what she'd given away.

Jake could only watch as everyone gathered around Nicole to praise the dance. Then they began to move away and gather their things while saying their good-byes. They recognized the undercurrents as well as he did, and they knew their presence was no longer appropriate.

The lyrics of the song made him remember those golden days

when they'd loved so freely. The first time they'd made love, Nicole's heartbeat had truly reminded him of a frightened bird, but she'd given herself without hesitation.

When he'd realized she had given her virginity as well, he had been filled with a kind of fearful pride. He'd been fearful that she hadn't received her full measure of pleasure, and full of pride that she'd trusted him to give her the first taste of physical fulfillment.

Yet he'd been selfish enough to ignore precautions, and they had both paid a price for their loving. In the end, it had cost them five years of separation. Maybe more, if he couldn't find some way to win Nicole back.

The memory of her intensity still burned his soul. The magic of that first time had never disappeared, even in the pain and disillusion of their breakup. Her dance had woven the same unforgettable magic, as though she, too, cherished what they'd shared.

He felt her gaze and looked up. His heart slammed against his ribs, then began pounding at an accelerated pace when he saw the vulnerability she couldn't hide. Her green eyes still glowed with the emotions that had moved her body and his soul.

He didn't notice when Brianna slipped off his lap to go with Maggie. Nor did he realize he'd crossed the room until he took Nicole's hands in his.

"Words fail me, Nicki. It was beautiful." He felt the tremors through her hands and tension shimmered around them. He knew he couldn't let the moment pass into uncertainty. "If I thought you meant what I felt while I watched you—"

"I did," Nicole spoke softly, her voice firm even though the fine trembling still telegraphed her emotions. "I want you to stay again tonight. This time with me."

His pulse resettled, throbbing low and insistent in response to her words. "I can't promise to go slow—"

"Neither can I."

Desire jolted through him and he fought the urge to crush her to him and satisfy the burning need that had filled him for weeks. Weeks? No, years . . . five years. "How long until Brianna is asleep?"

"It doesn't matter. Maggie will keep her tonight."

He glanced around the room. They were alone. The only thing that lingered was the faint aroma of their feast. He looked back to

Nicole and saw the steady light of decision in her eyes. He reached up to touch her mouth and her lips met his fingers. Their soft caress convinced him that the night he'd challenged her with had arrived.

He lifted her hand to his mouth, duplicated her gentle touch, then dampened her palm with his tongue. "If we don't go upstairs right now, anyone returning for forgotten dishes is going to be shocked."

"Somehow I don't think anyone will." Her smile teased him. "They seemed to have more important things to do than to worry about a few dishes they can pick up tomorrow."

"Well, in that case—" Jake tugged her into his arms and kissed her, thoroughly sampling her sweet flavor. He'd meant to bait her with the kiss, to test her confidence in her neighbors' discretion, but she held nothing back. The heat of it burned through his senses, leaving him short of breath when he finally pulled back.

Nicole's mouth, slightly parted and softly swollen from his kiss, sent Jake's blood surging until his entire body vibrated with need. Without another word, he turned toward the stairway and led her up to her apartment. He passed the couch with its promise of room for two. He wanted them to be one . . . and the single bed that didn't need to be made up would suffice.

In the bedroom, he ignored the light switch; the darkening dusk of early evening still offered enough light for them to find their way into each other's arms. As he held her, Jake breathed in the heady scent of Nicole mixed with the subtle fragrance she now wore. They kissed again, and their breath and tongues mingled while their hands stroked and caressed each other.

Nicole reached for the buttons on his shirt, then kissed the firm skin underneath, and Jake caught his breath.

"If we don't slow down, we'll burn ourselves up," he whispered. She kept undoing the buttons and pressing damp kisses against his chest as she worked. Jake tried to slow his breathing. "We need to savor this."

"I don't want to slow down. I want to feel the fire again."

Nicole brought her hands up to her hair and loosened the tight coil at the base of her neck. It flowed down her shoulders and back until the ends reached her waist. She combed her fingers through it, softening the severe lines until the dark brown strands shimmered in the twilight.

His pulse jerked, then hammered again. He loved the rich thickness of her hair. He smiled, trying to contain the predatory satisfaction of knowing she remembered that he delighted in the rich fall of her hair against his skin. He made himself step back before he gave into the impulse to take her where she stood.

He reached into his back pocket, pulling a foil packet from his wallet and placing it on the table beside the bed. "I've felt like such a Boy Scout on his best behavior for the last few weeks," he said. "I'm glad I remembered their motto."

"Do you know how to start a fire by rubbing things together?" Nicole teased him. "The kind of fire that burns fast and hot?"

"If the fire burns too fast, I'm liable to have a stroke before we go much further." He turned her around and slid the zipper of her dress down, then he slipped his hands around her waist inside the dress and pulled her back against him. "They say it's a great way to go, but I'd rather die afterward than during."

His hands played slowly over her rib cage, gliding with sensuous instinct, each stroke soothing and at the same time bringing Nicole's nerve endings alive with anticipation. When his hands traced the curve of her waist, he stopped, tightening them briefly around her before he wrapped his arms around the outside of her dress. "I want the buildup, the slow curling flames, and the explosive inferno that leaves us panting survivors."

He nuzzled her neck, sending waves of pleasure through her body. Did he know how often she'd dreamed he held her like this? When she caught the tang of wooded forest and aroused male, Nicole gave in to the heated current it stirred. No one else could ignite her the way he did.

She turned, standing only inches away, and watched his eyes while she let the sleek green cloth slide down to the floor. The quick dilation of his pupils told her he liked what the dress revealed. The sheer fabric of her lingerie hid nothing, and the fading window light highlighted the high slope of her breasts. He didn't move, though his gaze touched her so intently that her nipples grew taut with expectation.

Finally he reached up to trace the curve of one breast before cupping it in his hand and stroking its tip with his thumb. Nicole closed her eyes as pleasure washed over her. His left hand warmed her other breast and she let out a broken sigh. His hands stilled. She opened her eyes.

"Yes," he said. His voice held a note of husky satisfaction. "I want you to look at me when I touch you. I want to see your eyes darken with desire at the same time as I feel your skin heat and your pulse race."

He stroked his hands over her torso, first skimming, then stroking, lifting and teasing, as she stared into his eyes. Each touch shortened her breath with its gentle demand.

This was a Jake both familiar and new to her. The thrill of his hands on her body had haunted her dreams too often for her to forget his touch. Yet his touch had never made her feel quite so . . . cherished, before. His eyes had never held quite the same expression, either. Something in their depths made her heart sing just as the passion she recognized made her blood surge.

He released the front clasp of her bra and slowly brushed the straps from her shoulders. It fell to the floor unheeded as he brought his hands back to her bared flesh. A sensual flair of need sparked, then flamed, until Nicole could remain passive no longer but had to touch Jake with the same soul-mesmerizing rhythm she'd experienced.

She reached up and drew apart the shirt she'd unbuttoned earlier. Jake's eyes closed for just a half-second when her fingers brushed the taut flesh of his chest; then they snapped open again to let her see the heated pleasure her touch had returned.

He moved his hands to her hips and pulled her tighter against him, until she felt the evidence of his need. Nicole slipped her arms around Jake's lean waist, her fingers tracing each taut line of the corded muscles along his spine as she brushed his chest with her breasts and reveled in the pleasurable pressure of her hips against his.

How could she have forgotten how firm and hard his body was? Her dreams were little more than phantom memories when compared to the reality of the man who held her. She needed him. She had needed him for five years. She would always need him.

"Don't make me wait any more, Jake," she whispered. She tugged at his shirt, and he helped her pull it from the waistband of his slacks, and then she released the buckle on his belt. It took him only a moment to shed the rest of his clothes.

His muscles gleamed in the faint light, the tan from his Australian tour still contrasting strongly with the pale skin where his trunks had been. Strong, athletic legs supported his muscular frame before he pulled her down onto the bed beside him.

Jake stroked her as though touching her for the first time, exploring the intimate dips and rises of her body. His long fingers spread wide as he covered her, stroking and petting. She felt like a cat rising up to meet his hands.

His tongue teased her mouth again and again, encouraging her to take the lead. Excitement filled her as he coaxed, thrusting and parrying, until she answered by tasting him as deeply as he had tasted her. She caught the faint flavor of dinner wine as the warm interior of his mouth surrounded her tongue.

Her palms flattened against his firm shoulders, pulling them closer until she could feel the hammering of his heart against hers. Her fingertips traced his skin, the pads supersensitive to the fine contractions of his pulse as it raced to the rhythm of passion.

Her hands brushed the dark hair covering his chest, and its rough surface tickled her fingers, then her lips, as she kissed him. She didn't remember being so aware of the details about him before. She had taken the pleasure he gave her but had never been so aware of how he felt to her.

She moved a little higher, her nipples tingling as they brushed against the texture of his chest; then she touched the tip of her tongue to an intriguing spot at the base of his jaw.

"You taste so good," she whispered. She breathed in the scent of soap and musk as she ran her tongue along his earlobe, pulling it between her lips.

Jake made a hungry sound, then turned her so she lay halfway beneath him as he leaned over her. "Let me love you, Nicki," he murmured hoarsely. "Let me hear the little animal cries you used to make when I satisfied you."

His words made her shiver in anticipation as she remembered how fully he could satisfy her. Unable to remain passive when he aroused her, she could never stop the soft high mews of pleasure when he brought her to the peak of gratification. Nor could she ever stop the whimper of protest that escaped when they moved apart, even to nestle in each other's arms. The memory and expectation of that fulfillment again washed over her.

"Yes! Jake, hold me—love me."

Capturing her mouth for a brief instant of assurance, he traced a trail of kisses along her neck, down her shoulders and to her breasts. He brushed a finger lightly across their tips, then gathered them into his hands, gently squeezing, pressing, and massaging them until Nicole called his name.

"Did you want something?" he asked, his voice amused and low. "Something like this?"

He let his tongue circle her nipple, his breath cooling the surface before taking it into his mouth, warming it again as he suckled it. His hand continued to tease the other one while he made her thoroughly aware of how the velvet texture of his tongue could make her ache with need.

In all their time together she had never wanted him as much as she wanted him now. She'd waited too long, dreamed too many yearning dreams to stop or slow down. She wanted this. She wanted Jake.

He released her, raising his head to look with male satisfaction at the damply glistening pink flesh that seemed to pout at being abandoned. Nicole followed him up, then reached to guide his head back, and he gave a low laugh of exhilaration just before he followed her guidance and licked the other nipple. His mouth explored the second as thoroughly as the first. When he finally lifted his head again, Nicole moaned with pleasure.

"I never could get enough of you," he said. Taking her mouth for a brief, scorching moment, Jake trailed kisses back down her body, his probing hands leading the way.

The callused roughness of Jake's fingertips contrasted with the tenderness of his caress, and Nicole arched into his touch, relishing the sensations that spread throughout her body with every movement of his hands. He toyed with her, touching, stroking, teasing until she wanted to pull him down onto her, into her.

When she tried, he resisted with a low laugh that sent her blood surging faster. "Not yet, Nicki," he whispered. "I'm not done stoking the flames yet. I want you to melt me with your fire."

His hands slid down her hips and thighs, then circled around and skimmed the sensitive flesh inside her legs until he reached the dark triangle where they joined. He brushed his knuckles lightly across the soft hair before letting his palm cup her. His possession sent her breath rushing from her as heat spiraled up through her body. When he slowly rotated his hand, his fingers pressing lightly into her warmth, she gasped his name again as pleasure rose deep within her.

"Yes! Call me, Nicki. Tell me how much you want my touch."

Nicole tried to answer, but her voice tangled with the panting breaths she drank in short gulps. When he bent his head to brush his lips along her inner thigh, she thought she might truly melt with need. Her body throbbed, pulsing with anticipation, aching with emptiness that only Jake could fill.

He touched her core and the flames leapt, burning through her, paralyzing her lungs as she drowned in sensation and liquid heat. After an eternity in paradise, her body pulled in a gasp of air, and mindless cries, high, soft and keening, escaped until her breath slowed its frantic pace.

Jake's voice held a rough edge of desire. "I love to pleasure you." He let his mouth rove gently and slowly back up her body until he reached her lips. "You almost take me with you when you soar away." After a minute, he eased back, pulling Nicole with him until she lay over him, half covering him with her body as he had hers. "Now pleasure me, Nicki. Take me to the edge so we can fly together."

Nine

Tiny fissures of pleasure still shimmered in her veins as Nicole leaned down and kissed him. She savored the warm firmness of his lips, the hot seduction of his mouth. She shifted, rising up so that her breasts brushed against the firm wall of his chest, her nipples tight as they touched his. Their hypersensitive nerve endings sent new messages of anticipation into her core. Jake released a low growl of approval as Nicole moved slowly, keeping their contact tantalizingly light.

With returning fervor, she dipped her head and followed the line of his body with her lips, stopping occasionally to let her tongue explore the contrasting textures of his skin. At the side of his waist she found skin as tender and smooth as a child's, along his belly a fine hair-roughened tautness that sent her pulse racing again. He tasted faintly of salt and something indefinably Jake.

Stroking him, tasting him, made her forget everything. She was no one's mother, no one's daughter. She was Jake's lover. Her skin against his made his breathing falter then race; her mouth against his made damp paths across the faint sheen of moisture that now covered both their bodies. When she ran her hands over the firm flesh, trailing her nails lightly from his ribs to his hips, he called her name and arched into her hands. He made her feel as no one ever had: wild, wanton, and wanted. She stroked his proud flesh until he stilled her hands with his.

"Don't pleasure me too much, Nicki, or we won't fly together." His voice betrayed the effort it took to hold back.

Nicole drew away long enough to take the small packet from the table. She didn't need to wait. Her body throbbed with readiness, a tangible ache only he could satisfy. She wanted to have Jake inside her, filling her. Having sheathed him with protection, she needed to sheathe him with her body.

He shifted her beneath him again, then rubbed his arousal against her with a low growl of pleasure. Nicole lifted her hips to meet him, catching her breath when he entered her at last. Her breath came out a sigh, then caught again when he moved with slow, measured thrusts that sent rivers of heat coursing through her body.

Nicole let her hands rove Jake's chest and belly, her eyes closed as she swam in a sea of sensation. She moved her knees up high, pulling him in deeper. He grasped her hips, helping her as he began moving faster. Ripples and swirls of multicolored fire made kaleidoscope patterns across her eyelids, and she clung to him, urging him on.

The explosion of joy came to them both, and the kaleidoscope shattered into a rainbow of brilliant shards, their gold and crimson crystals filling Nicole with fissures of light.

Satiated, they lay wrapped in each other's arms. Jake pulled her more tightly against him, his hand cupping her breast with tender possession. "It's still there, Nicki."

The fire faded slowly until it became a warm glow of satisfaction, and Nicole nestled closely. He brushed his lips over her shoulder, and Nicole let her eyes drift closed. Jake's gentle breath caressed her neck, and by its slowed steadiness she knew he dozed contentedly beside her. She dozed, waking before Jake.

The moonlight lent its shadowed illumination, allowing her to study the large brown hand that still held her to him even in his sleep. She had to think. Now that Jake no longer overwhelmed practical thought, Nicole needed to face the consequences of letting her heart and body rule her mind again. He was right. They still struck fire from one another . . . and once the flame began, she was powerless to put it out by any other means.

She had instinctively known this from the moment he had reentered her life, yet she let it happen . . . had wanted it to happen. Why else had she visited the drugstore and purchased her own supply of protection that now rested, unopened in the drawer of the bed table? She had known. Now what did she do about it?

For the moment she didn't have to decide. She would take the rest of the night with Jake and not let herself worry about what she ought to do, what she wanted to do, or even if there was anything she could do.

Jake stirred, his hand lazily stroking her bare skin, and warm desire began to move through her again. His fingers sliding over her hips, her rib cage, her belly, sent threads of anticipation through her body, drawing her nerves into fine tune. Her breath released in a soft sigh, and she pressed closer into his embrace, every inch of her flesh aware of the masculine strength that held her.

"You smell good," he whispered in her ear. "Like clean soap and satisfied woman."

Jake stretched, then dropped his arm back down to keep Nicole's body next to his. He savored the way her back pressed against his belly and hips, the curve of her derriere fitting perfectly against him when he drew his legs up, spoon fashion, under hers.

He admitted to himself that he'd never given up the dream of holding Nicole like this again. He'd told himself that his search for her was necessary so he could close the door on the past and move on to a life with no regrets, but he'd known that he wanted this one more time. Now that he had, he wanted it forever.

He brushed his hand over the contour of Nicole's breast, its silky resilience causing his body to stir, and he chuckled in delight. "You have an amazing effect on my body," he whispered into her ear.

"I haven't recovered my . . . uh . . . interest this quickly since I was twenty."

"I guess thinking like a Boy Scout made you feel as young as one," Nicole responded.

"Too bad I'm not better prepared," he said, as he shifted to a less intimate position. "I only brought one."

Nicole chuckled and shifted with him, maintaining the contact he'd tried to break.

"I understand they let girls into the troops now."

Jake groaned when she moved with him. "Honey, I'm trying to protect you."

Nicole rubbed her backside against Jake's lap before breaking away to sit on the edge of the bed. She opened the drawer and removed the small box. Turning back to him, she put the box into his hand. "I always admired Boy Scouts," she said. "Do you think you could build another fire with these?"

The moonlight lit his grin of surprise. Then he reached out and pulled her down to capture her mouth in a hot kiss. "If I can't," he muttered against her lips, "I'll turn in my merit badges."

The practicalities of life faded, and Jake made love to her until they finally lay exhausted and replete.

The faint light of pre-dawn woke Jake first, and for several minutes he lay still, his hand absorbing the soft fullness of Nicole's breast. This time he wasn't surprised when he felt the familiar surge of desire that centered itself against Nicole's thigh.

A glance at the clock beside the bed told him he needed to shower and leave quickly if he was going to make his flight out of the local airport. Reluctantly, he eased himself from the bed.

"Jake?" Nicole stirred immediately, even through the heavy fog of sleep.

"It's all right, sweetheart," Jake whispered as he pulled the blankets high to protect her from the morning chill. "I'm just going to take a shower."

He couldn't resist kissing her just once more before heading into the bathroom. Her lips were warm and inviting, tempting him to consider a later plane, but he had no choice. His flight from New York to London was timed too close for that kind of delay. His mouth twitched in grim humor as he adjusted the knobs in the bathroom. After last night, he hadn't thought he'd be taking another cold shower.

Nicole stirred, her hand seeking Jake's hard body. When she encountered empty space she opened her eyes. For a split second she felt the sharp pain that followed her hungry dreams of the past. Then she heard the shower running, and the hazy warmth of Jake's kiss when he left the bed floated back to her.

She sat up, more aware of her body than she'd been in years. Dancing kept her muscles too supple for her to feel stiff, but they resonated with vibrant tone. Jake was a master musician with more than a guitar. He made her body harmonize with her soul until she became a love song in his arms.

Nicole heard the shower shut off as she stood up and reached for her robe. She slipped it on and began picking up the clothes they'd shed the night before, trying to keep her mind blank. Jake would be leaving within the hour, and when he returned the realities of everyday life would bring them back to their senses.

Jake opened the bathroom door, and Nicole caught her breath at the beauty of his body. His voice held a wealth of warm memory when he wished her good morning. Suddenly flustered, she cursed herself for the flush she felt creep up her skin.

"I'll make you some coffee while you get dressed."

Amusement laced his voice as he stepped into his briefs. "Will you blush like that when we get married?"

Nicole froze, the warm fluttery feeling replaced by cold shock. "I thought I'd made myself clear, Jake. I don't intend to marry you. If having great sex or being pregnant were the only reasons for getting married we would have been married a long time ago."

"We could have been, Nicki," Jake shot back. "You ran away, I didn't."

"If I hadn't, we would have ended up hating each other. I made a choice." Nicole turned away from Jake's sudden fury. She should have known the beauty of their night would evaporate in the morning.

"As for last night, don't get the idea that what happened was the result of some diabolical plan of yours that I couldn't resist.

And don't," she warned him, her voice harsh with pain, "think for a minute that it was anything more than a physical thing. Women are capable of lust, too. I find you overwhelmingly attractive, but it takes more than sex to make a marriage work, and that's all we have."

Jake let loose a barnyard expletive. "What kind of Victorian malarkey is that? If I was only interested in your mind I might as well be your brother."

He closed the distance between them, turning her to face him again. "We lived together for six months before you left, Nicole. How was that different from being married? We talked, we laughed, we argued . . . and we made a baby."

He ran his hands through his hair, then leveled his gaze at her as though pinning her to the wall. "As for the sex, you can't tell me you melt like that with every other man you've ever slept with. Sex without feelings is never that incredible."

"Feelings?" Nicole laughed harshly as a shaft of pain lanced through her. "That's a pretty bland word. What does it mean?" she scoffed. "That we're not strangers who pay for the privilege?"

"I love you, dammit," Jake ground out. "Is that a good enough word? And what's more, I think you love me."

His words only inflamed Nicole more. She didn't need empty phrases to give validity to the passion they'd shared.

"Don't give me some line about love, Jake. You've never mentioned it before—not even last night when you were whispering the most intimate observations and suggestions. You didn't love me when we were living together and you don't love me now. You just want Brianna—and you don't object to the bed partner who comes with her."

Jake stilled, and the air around them seemed to crackle with the shock reflected in his eyes. Too softly he asked, "Is that what you really think of me?"

Was it? Hearing her fears voiced so bluntly, she wondered how much she believed them. "I . . . no."

"Then why say it?" Jake brought his hands up and settled them on Nicole's shoulders. "Nicki, I won't deny that I want Brianna or that getting married would simplify everything. But whether you believe me or not, I do love you."

Nicole didn't answer. She couldn't. Her heart wanted to believe him, but her practical mind balked. His words had come too quickly, and only after she'd taunted him.

When she didn't answer, Jake dropped his hands and stepped back. "I've got to leave in a few minutes, honey. I don't want to leave things unsettled like this, but if I don't leave now I'll miss my flight." He ran a hand through his damp hair. "But when I get back, I promise I'll find a way to convince you that I meant what I said."

He pulled on his shirt and reached for his slacks. "Just promise me you won't run away again while I'm gone."

"I won't run," Nicole assured him. "I don't need to anymore."

Nicole and Brianna stood on the sidewalk while Jake loaded his guitar into one of the two vans that waited with his crew. Closing the door in the back, he turned to say good-bye.

"I'll be landing at L.A.X. on Christmas Eve morning," he told her soberly. "Traffic will be even worse down there, so don't look for me to get out here until at least three in the afternoon . . . but I'll be here."

Jake hated to leave. Nicole had backed down from her accusations of the morning, but she had believed them in some part of her mind, he was sure. It was too soon for him to leave after she had lowered her defenses. Three weeks was too long.

"Jake! Hurry up and kiss her good-bye so we can get out of here," George called out with a laugh.

The others added their own encouragements, and Jake turned back to Nicole. "I guess they're right." Catcalls and amused hooting erupted from the van when Jake took George's advice. He pulled her into his arms, holding her fiercely for a moment before kissing her deeply. He wanted to brand her as his. When he raised his head again he whispered, "Wait for me."

Releasing her, he knelt down and gathered Brianna into his arms. He didn't want to leave her behind either. She had insinuated herself into his life so completely in such a short time. Having a daughter still filled him with awe. It was too new to let go of. He gave her a warm hug and a gentle kiss before running a stroking caress along her cheek. "Good-bye, Brianna," he signed.

To his surprise, Brianna burst into tears and began signing frantically. "What's she saying?" He turned to Nicole. "She's signing too fast for me to understand."

"She doesn't want you to go. She's afraid you won't come back." Nicole knelt down beside Jake. "Daddy is coming back. He'll be here for Christmas. Santa will bring his presents here for him."

Only slightly reassured, Brianna's chubby hands moved again, a little slower than before. Seeing the pained guilt that filtered over Nicole's face as she read Brianna's signs, Jake demanded impatiently, "What is it? What's she saying?"

"She says you went away before she was born, and you're going away again."

"Help me explain, Nicole," Jake implored. "Tell her what I'm saying." He faced Brianna as he held his right hand up. His thumb, forefinger, and pinky were extended while his middle and ring fingers touched his palm. "I love you, Brianna. When I went away before, you hadn't been born yet. But I know you now . . . and I love you. I'm coming back just as soon as I can. I promise." Gathering her into his arms, Jake hugged Brianna tightly before letting her go to search her face for understanding.

Pain twisted Nicole's heart when she saw that his eyes had misted, their sapphire colored depths blazing with sincerity. Brianna touched his face the way he had done earlier.

"Daaa-dee."

Jake jerked as though he'd touched a live wire, and his eyes and nose stung as he tried to take air into his lungs. His heart pounded as he heard the hesitant sound of his daughter's voice for the first time.

"Ah-ee luv you."

Suddenly shy, she buried her face into his shirt, and Jake's arms closed around her while his heart swelled with joy. He bowed his head over hers, absorbing the sweet little girl scents of powder, soap, and chocolate milk. Never had he hated clocks and airline schedules more.

Finally, Brianna shifted, and Jake released her. The grin on his face made her giggle. Her hands moved quickly, then she moved next to her mother, half hiding behind her.

"She says, 'I'll see you at Christmas.' "

He stood. "Take care of yourselves." He hesitated, not wanting to go but knowing he had no choice. Finally, he turned and walked quickly to the van.

As the vans pulled out onto the street, Nicole and Brianna waved, not stopping until the vehicles had turned the corner out of sight.

"Great, David!" Nicole called from her vantage point at the back of the auditorium. "You'll knock them out of their seats."

David bowed to her in response, then disappeared behind the side curtains toward the landing that led to the dressing rooms. The final dress rehearsal would begin when the orchestra members arrived in an hour and a half, and Nicole had been hard at work since noon. With David having finished a final run-through of his solo variation, she needed to check one more scene before getting into costume herself.

She turned her head left and called out, "Harry, I think the spotlight is too dim, could you check it?"

A man's voice responded from the side of the stage near a huge panel of toggle switches and blinking lights. A muffled *"Aha!"* floated from the unseen entity just before the spotlight in question beamed to life again, brighter than before.

"I don't know what you did, but you fixed it," Nicole called. "Thanks."

The local college auditorium they rented for these productions allowed seating for twelve hundred, the perfect size for a local studio. The slope of the aisles was steep enough to allow a good view from every seat, and the stage was new enough that there were no worn spots that might trip up her dancers. The rental fee included the lighting and stage crew from the drama department, which saved Nicole the added headache of hiring separately.

She contracted with the local symphony for two night performances each year, using a tape for the Sunday matinee. Nicole liked this arrangement, since the orchestra added to the professional environment she tried to create for her pupils. If things went well this year, she hoped to stretch her production into two weekends next Christmas.

"Are the mice and soldiers ready for their run-through?" She clapped her hands briskly. "Hurry up. This is our last chance before the orchestra starts warming up. Mark! Lori! Where are you? We're waiting."

Eight little girls, ranging in age from six to ten and dressed in brown tights and multicolored leotards, assembled themselves on stage. Black dancing slippers graced their feet, instead of the usual pink, so they would blend with the shaggy brown mouse costumes they'd wear during the dress rehearsal in another hour. With them were eight other children of similar age, both boys and girls, dressed in white tights and already wearing the bright red and gold jackets of tin soldiers. The mouse costumes were so hot, particularly under the bright lights, that the mice waited until the last minute before suiting up. Three mothers waited backstage to help them.

Mark, a blond boy slightly older and taller than the others, arrived at last. He played the Nutcracker/Prince in the production.

"I'm sorry, Nicole," he called. "We couldn't find my mask." He held up the latex plastic nutcracker mask that he wore during the battle scene. Lori, who played Clara, stood beside him in the white nightgown that was her costume.

"Well, now that you're here, let's get started. Places, everyone."

On stage, the backdrops created a regal living room from the past. In the center back of the stage a magnificent Christmas tree set the season. Two huge boxes, deep rose red and painted to give the illusion of Christmas presents, hid the crouched bodies of four mice. A lace-draped table beside the tree acted as a screen where Mark waited for the mysterious Herr Dresslemier to change the small wooden nutcracker into a living one.

She pushed the button on the tape and waited. From the front, the stage looked empty of life as the thin, reedy-pitched music began. Soon, however, a full battle raged between the troops of the King Rat and the Nutcracker's soldiers over the possession of the packages under the tree.

A soldier rode a broom-handled horse across the stage to be met by a mouse who pushed him aside and claimed it for herself. A line of troops marched briskly across the stage, silver-painted swords gleaming in the bright lights. The King Rat leapt in front of the Nutcracker only to be mortally wounded by the slipper Clara threw at him. The mouse troops vanquished, they sadly pulled their fallen leader off stage while the Nutcracker rose up, transformed into the Prince.

Nicole shut off the tape recorder. "Good work, kids," she praised them. "Now go do your homework until you're on. Remember," she continued, "no eating in costume."

She checked her clipboard to make sure she hadn't forgotten anything when Maggie tapped her on the shoulder.

"Just so you follow your own rules, here's your dinner. Now eat it before you change."

Nicole reached into the bag Maggie handed her and pulled out a large, oozing bean burrito and a package of onion rings. Maggie always complained that the fast food Nicole lived on through production season ought to make her sick or fat or both. Still, Maggie made sure Nicole ate something, even if she disapproved of what it was.

"Jake called," she announced as she handed Nicole a small stack of messages to be clipped to the board. "He said to tell you that bad dress rehearsals mean a good performance. But if everything went smoothly tonight, I'm to tell you that a good dress rehearsal means a better performance." She gave a gravelly chuckle. "I wasn't supposed to tell you he called until after I saw how things went."

Nicole laughed. Leave it to Maggie to say things up front.

"He also said to tell you he would call you tomorrow after opening night."

The few days Jake had been gone had made Nicole realize how much she'd become used to having him in her life again. She'd forgotten how his presence could make her aware of her blood humming through her body or how she noticed little things like the everyday scents and colors of life. He brought her to life just by walking into the studio, and though that fact worried her, it excited her at the same time.

She missed him.

The new Jake was less driven now that he had his full measure of the success he had craved before. He showed a greater patience for things he couldn't control. She knew how much he wanted to make up for the time he'd lost with Bri. Yet no matter how trying it must have been for him to understand Bri, or to wait until she was ready, he'd worked to gain her trust and affection.

Now that Brianna had spoken to him, Nicole knew he would press even more for her to marry him. He'd told Nicole that he loved her, yet before their argument he had never said anything to indicate that his love extended to her in the same way as it did to Brianna.

He was thoughtful and generous, and he wanted her. He made that clear. He also wanted to be Brianna's legal father. But he never spoke of marriage as anything but the right thing to do. Nicole frowned. Damn it, she refused to be salve for his conscience.

"You've got that expression again," Maggie interrupted her thoughts. "And you're not eating your dinner."

"What expression?" She took a huge bite of burrito.

"Actually, it has two forms," Maggie clarified. "First you get all dreamy . . . the kind of expression that embarrasses prudes and interests most men. Then it shifts through sadness to something like Attila the Hun getting ready to scale the walls of a city."

Nicole's eyes opened wide in shock at Maggie's description. "What's that supposed to mean?"

"That means, my dear, that you love him, you want him, but for some strange reason I'll never understand, you won't let yourself keep him." She patted Nicole's arm. "Don't worry. You can always change your mind." She hesitated, then added gently, "Until he gives up trying to change it."

Nicole looked at Maggie in surprise. Had she been that transparent? Maggie's last words worried her. Yet wasn't that what Nicole wanted? For Jake to stop trying to change her mind about marriage and accept just being Brianna's father? Would that ever really be what she wanted?

She frowned as another thought struck her. What if he married someone else? When he had been a distant figure from her past, the idea had caused her some pain, but a distant pain. What would it be like meeting his wife face to face? Or seeing the two of them taking her daughter for visits? A knife thrust of pain burned through her, and she blanched at the thought.

"Nicole, dear," Maggie broke in to her distressing thoughts. "I didn't mean to upset you so much. After all, Jake doesn't strike me as the kind of man who gives up easily. If the thought bothers you that much, all you have to do is stop fighting him."

Nicole tore her mind away from her fears and forced a smile.

"I'm afraid it's a little more complicated than it appears, Maggie. I can't marry him on his terms, okay?"

It was Maggie's turn to stare in amazement. "What do you mean 'his terms'? Does he want one of those open marriages?"

"Of course not." Nicole had to laugh. Jake didn't share some things. "Just take my word for it. I can't marry him." The door at the side of the auditorium opened, and the conductor came in, followed by the first of the orchestra members. Their arrival reminded Nicole of the time, and she crumpled the remains of her dinner into the bag. "I've got to go change, Maggie." She was glad for an excuse to drop the discussion.

The clock in the studio lobby read well past midnight before Nicole and David climbed tiredly up the back stairs to Nicole's apartment.

"Lord, I'm glad I'm not driving back to L.A. tonight," David said. "I'd have gotten home just in time to turn around and come back." He shifted a sleeping Brianna in his arms. "Of course, if I'd had any sense, I wouldn't have volunteered to do anything except dance. Then I could have slept in my own bed until late afternoon if I'd wanted, instead of braving your hide-a-bed and getting up by nine to look for missing props and act as delivery boy for programs."

Nicole dug into her bag and located her key. "Give it up, David," she said. "You've done this every year, and you love it."

She looked back at him as they crossed the threshold and had to grin when he admitted, "Only after it's all done and the adrenaline is still in force. Right now I'm ready to drop and not move for a week."

A yawn caught her. "I hear you."

Nicole took Bri from David and headed for her room before the door shut behind her. When David wished her good night, she only nodded and stifled another yawn. Brianna slept soundly, not even stirring when Nicole gave her a soft kiss and tucked her in. She had fallen asleep in the dressing room long before they'd finished their lock-up.

The insistent ringing of the phone roused Nicole long before she was ready to wake. Fighting her way through the sleepy fog that dulled her brain, she reached for the extension beside her bed. She mumbled acknowledgment into the receiver.

"Rise and shine, sleepyhead," Jake's voice was disgustingly cheerful and held the same teasing note it had on Thanksgiving morning.

She sat up and looked at the clock and groaned when she focused on the numbers. "Do you know what time it is?"

"Sure, it's two-thirty in the afternoon here in London, so it's seven-thirty in the morning your time."

"It is not seven-thirty here, you fool," she told him bluntly. She fell back against the pillows again. "It is only six-thirty. There is an eight hour difference from London to California." She closed her eyes. "Besides, what makes you think I wanted to be up at seven-thirty, either?"

"I'm sorry, Nicki." An undercurrent of laughter took some of the sincerity out of his apology. "I really thought I'd timed things well."

"Well, you didn't." Nicole tried to sound disgruntled, but his amusement could tease her even from England.

"Is Bri up yet?"

Nicole checked the bed on the opposite wall and answered without thinking. "She's not in her bed, so she must be in the living room pestering David."

An electric silence followed. Finally Jake spoke again, the teasing warmth of a few minutes ago now encased in ice. "What's David doing there at six in the morning . . . or need I ask?"

Ten

"He's sleeping in the living room," she retorted sharply. "Didn't you hear me?"

"Yes, but where did you sleep?"

"That's my business." If Jake still had the idea that she and David were anything more than friends, especially after the way she'd made love with him, she refused to dignify his suspicions with a denial. "Now mind your own business and let me go back to sleep!" She slammed the receiver back into its cradle then rolled over hugging her pillow, burying her face in it. *Damn him!*

Awake now, she couldn't get back to sleep. *He did the same thing to me at Thanksgiving.* She cursed him again as she headed for the kitchen to make a pot of coffee, zipping the front of her robe as she did.

"Who was that at this hour?" David's sleepy voice mumbled beyond the arm of the sofa.

"Jake. He had his times mixed up." *And his facts, too,* she mentally added.

At the door of the kitchen, Nicole stopped, then wailed in dismay, "Oh, Bri! Why today?"

Brianna sat at the table, her soft pink blanket sleepers coated in dark brown chocolate mix. The table also showed large piles of spilled chocolate powder, and Brianna's face was obscured by an equally dark moustache. The tall glass she held still contained a few drops of chocolate milk. Two huge blue eyes, the color of her father's, shone with triumph. "Ah-ee made choc-lat," she said clearly.

Nicole lowered her head in defeat. "I give up," she muttered to herself. "She's just like her father. I can't stay mad at him, either."

Nicole hurried around the rest of the morning. She and David shifted props that had been forgotten the night before. She checked with the box office for the latest ticket count and did a hundred and one other energy consuming tasks that accompanied a ballet opening night.

The dressing rooms buzzed with the excited chatter of her students by the time Nicole finally sat down to put on her makeup. A partition separated the makeup area from the actual dressing area, so that most of the bustle remained out of sight of the door that had been propped open in the name of practicality and fresh air.

People flowed in and out of the room in a beehive of activity. The room steamed with the mingled aromas of dust, perfume, greasepaint, and hairspray. Anticipation heated the air, and Nicole breathed it in with a smile.

She drew an exaggerated narrow black line along her eyelid just as David called her name. "I'll be right there," she answered as she painted a matching line above the other lid.

The heady fragrance of roses filled the room as she turned around. David stuck his head around one of the most unique bouquets Nicole had ever seen. It held one of every color rose she thought existed.

"You'd think with all his money he could have ordered something that matched." He grinned and handed Nicole the card.

Nicole opened it with trembling fingers.

My only excuse for waking you is that time isn't passing fast enough until the tour is finished and I can come home again. Tradition says each color rose has special meaning in the language of love. I didn't want to miss telling you all my thoughts.

Break a leg,
Jake

She blinked to keep the sting of greasepaint from being washed into her eyes. She reached out and stroked the delicate pink petal of one of the buds. Rich scent floated into the air, momentarily overcoming the cacophony of aromas that had filled the space seconds before. Jake had never been content with the expected. Two more weeks stretched until she saw him again.

"Don't start crying," David teased. "Greasepaint burns like fire if you get it in your eyes—and you don't have time do your makeup over. Curtain's in twenty minutes."

After the performance, half the audience seemed to swarm backstage to congratulate each of the performers. Long after the last parent and child left, Nicole worked to make sure everything was accounted for and in its place. A missing key to lock up the theater meant another hour's search and another hour's wait before security could lock everything for them. Ironically, when she picked her purse up to leave, the missing key fell to the floor, though she'd searched the purse three times. She and David finally climbed the stairs to her apartment at two-thirty in the morning.

"Don't wake me until noon," she told David as she disappeared into her room.

"I'd have to be awake myself, before I could do that," David answered as he stifled a yawn.

"God bless you, Maggie." Nicole sighed as she looked at Brianna's empty bed. Her neighbor had suggested Brianna be allowed to stay at her apartment tonight so Nicole could sleep in after the opening night performance.

She set Jake's flowers on the dresser and stopped to inhale their sweet perfume one more time before changing into a soft flannel gown. She crawled gratefully between the sheets and immediately fell into the heavy, dreamless slumber of exhaustion.

The shrill ringing of the telephone jerked Nicole out of her sleep for the second night in a row. Fumbling, she knocked a box of tissues onto the floor, then finally grabbed the receiver. "Damn it, Jake, not again! Flowers or no flowers, I just got to bed," she glanced at the clock, "two hours ago—"

"Nicole, it isn't Jake. It's Val. Val Lassiter."

Nicole blinked and wondered why Pete's wife would call her at four in the morning.

"Nicole, I have some bad news . . ."

Fear wiped away any trailing cobwebs of sleep, and Nicole gripped the receiver tightly. "What's happened. Is Jake hurt?"

"We don't know. There's been a fire at Jake's hotel. Pete just called me. He was across town at a meeting when it happened, but Jake was—" Val's voice broke and Nicole closed her eyes as a wave of nausea threatened to overwhelm her.

Val came back on the line. "We don't know that he's been hurt. Only that he was at the hotel, and we haven't been able to locate him. There's so much confusion. It was the middle of the lunchtime rush." She didn't say anything for a moment, then added, "I wish I could tell you more."

Nicole sat numbly staring at the wall, while she broke into little pieces inside. Words seemed to bounce around in her head, taunting her. Fire . . . Jake . . . don't know . . . Vaguely, she heard a woman's voice calling her name. She knew the woman wanted her to answer but she couldn't. Nicole had no vocal cords, no logical understanding, only a searing, tearing pain that wiped out all else.

Blindly, automatically, she placed the receiver back on its cradle. Then, she got out of bed and walked to the bouquet on the dresser. Her movements were jerky, as disjointed as her thoughts. She selected a delicate lavender rose and pulled it slowly from the arrangement, and held its velvet petals against her cheek. The telephone began pealing again but she paid it no attention as she made her way into the living room through the darkness of the pre-dawn morning.

The phone's insistent ringing finally stopped when David woke up and answered it. Nicole ignored him as she pulled out a CD and put it in the player. She pushed the right buttons and Jake's low voice wove through the room.

"Hello?" David mumbled, half asleep. "This is David Cole. Yeah, her friend, why?"

Nicole watched him as though staring at a television screen, detached and unflinching. David sat up suddenly. He turned to look at Nicole. "Oh, my God. Yes, I'll take care of her," he assured Val. "Look, she's pretty dazed, I'd better go. Call if you get any word."

He hung up without wasting time on good-byes. He hurried to where Nicole stood beside the stereo cabinet, stroking her fingers over the pictured image on the album cover she held. The guitar cords of Jake's first album floated softly from the speakers.

"He's dead, David," Nicole's voice sounded hollow and flat. She stared at him, her words formed as stiffly as her movements had been. "Jake is dead . . . fire . . . the hotel—"

David came to stand beside her, his hand on her shoulder. "You don't know that."

"He was there."

"Nicole!" David shook her, his voice sharp, forcing itself into her shocked mind. "Listen to me. He's probably just fine. Just because Pete hasn't located him doesn't mean he's dead—or even hurt."

Nicole's body began to shake and her green eyes filled with tears. "I don't think I could stand it if . . ." A wrenching sob broke free, and she buried her face against David's chest. When the wracking sobs quieted to an occasional sniffing shudder, she drew back from the shelter of David's brotherly embrace.

"No matter what happens you'll be able to handle it, Nicole. You did when it was Cathy, and you did when it was Brianna. You will now." He chucked her lightly under the chin. "He'll be all right, Nicole. Jake's as strong and stubborn as you are."

Startled out of her shock, Nicole studied David's face carefully. It was the first time he had mentioned Cathy in six years. Cathy had been the victim of a disease she'd brought on herself; her friend had starved herself for her career.

"Does it still hurt you to think about her?"

David looked surprised, as though making a discovery. "No. I wish I'd known what was going on soon enough to save her, but the pain is gone. Time is the greatest healer."

"I thought time had cured me of loving Jake, but—"

Nicole turned and started pacing the living room. "I have to do something David. I can't just sit and wait, not knowing anything. I've got to find out—"

"There isn't anything you can do," David argued gently. "Pete will call as soon as—"

"I can call London. I can check with the hospitals." Now that her tears were spent, she felt a restlessness that would not let her stop until she discovered the truth.

"Do you know how many people will be calling the hospitals? Which hospital would you call? There's certainly more than one hospital in London, you know."

"The police will know where the injured have been taken. I'll call the London police and then—"

"Nicole! Listen to me! The police will be swamped with calls. Even if you could get through to them they wouldn't be able to give you information." David hesitated, then took Nicole's arm, drawing her over to the couch and making her sit down.

"Look." He sighed. "Suppose you got through to the police. Even suppose that they gave you the names of the hospitals where he might be. Then what?"

Nicole stared up at him in confusion, "I'd call the hospital and ask if—"

"Right," David interrupted. "You'd ask them if Jake is there. They'd ask who wants to know. You'd tell them Nicole Michaels. They'd ask if you're a relative . . ." David gave Nicole a pitying look as he made his point. "You'd say, not really, but . . . and some polite nurse will say she is sorry but she can't give out any information over the telephone." He leaned down, putting his hands on her shoulders, and looking directly into her eyes. "I hate to say it, love, but in the eyes of the world you don't have the right to know anything about him or his condition."

"But he's Brianna's father, surely—"

"That's what you say," he said bluntly.

Nicole started up from the couch, and David held her down, soothing her anger.

"Hold it. I know Jake is her father. You know Jake is her father. Even Jake knows that he's her father. But, and this is a very important but, the nurse doesn't know that Jake is her father. His private life is well known. Everyone knows he's never been married. If Bri had been born after he became famous, you can bet that some enterprising reporter would have found out. But even Jake didn't know for sure until three weeks ago.

"Unfortunately, the public record is all that matters. There will be too much confusion for the hospital to listen to explanations even if they believed them. I'm sorry, Nicole," he said again. "There's nothing you can do right now, but wait."

Nicole sagged into the cushions, leaning her head back against the headrest, and resigned herself to wait. "You've made your point, David."

Dawn broke slowly as Nicole, wrapped in a blanket against the morning chill, stared at the television screen waiting for the early morning news. While she waited, cartoon characters chased each other across the screen, and Nicole fidgeted.

At last the screen cleared and the newscast's logo appeared. She reached over to turn the sound up just as the announcer said, "—exploded in a London hotel a few hours ago at the peak of lunch hour traffic. In Washington, the President met with representatives from the Coalition for Economic Reforms . . . and in Tennessee, miners threaten to walk out if the latest contract negotiations fail to bring more substantial improvements in safety regulations and health benefits. We'll have these stories and more, when we return."

David came to stand beside her, his hand squeezing her shoulder in support. "Hang in there, Nicole."

The announcer returned after several commercials and Nicole leaned forward tensely as he began filling in the lead stories.

"A toxic gas leak caused a huge explosion and fire in London's prestigious Royal Arms Hotel today. The explosion shook the entire block shortly after noon, a time when pedestrian traffic and business luncheons were at their peak. So far, at least eight people are known dead, though the figure is expected to go much higher as firemen sift through the rubble. The explosion was centered just below the main lobby near the first floor restaurant, and damage estimates are well over a million American dollars. Singer-composer, Jake Cameron, on tour during the holiday season, is known to have been staying at the Royal Arms and is missing, but it is not known if he was in the hotel at the time of the blast."

The camera shifted to the co-anchor woman as she began a new story, and David stood up to turn off the television.

"No news is good news," he mumbled dryly.

The phone rang, and Nicole leaped from the chair, throwing off the cumbersome blanket.

"Hello?" Her face fell and she answered the caller. "Yes, Maggie, I know. His manager's wife called me a few hours ago. We still don't know any more than we did then. I'm waiting to hear from them so . . ." Her voice trailed off, and Maggie took the hint. "I'll let you know when I hear from London."

Mr. Rosen had been watching the early morning news, as well. Again Nicole repeated what she knew and hurriedly freed the line. Well-meaning friends continued to call, and David took over, asking the callers to spread the word to those who had not. Even so, nearly an hour passed before the phone became silent.

Time dragged then. Nicole didn't want to talk, and David let her sit quietly. Her eyes felt gritty and dried out after she had cried away all her tears, and the headache that pulsed at her temples had more to do with fear than sleeplessness. She hadn't realized she'd dozed until the phone's shrill ring jerked her awake. Terror clutched at her heart as she lunged for the receiver.

"We found him, Nicole. He's in the hospital, but he's okay."

Nicole lowered her head. "Thank you, Lord," she whispered brokenly.

"Nicole, are you still there?"

"Yes, I'm here. How is he? Why is he in the hospital? How badly is he hurt?"

"We still don't know how badly he's hurt. He was unconscious when they brought him in, but no one recognized him without his beard and he didn't have any ID on him. With all the confusion they just assigned him a 'John Doe' until they took care of the worst cases. I guess he finally regained consciousness and was able to tell them who he was."

Nicole saw David hovering beside her and she covered the

mouthpiece to tell him, "Why don't you get on the extension?" She turned her attention back to Val. "What was that?"

"The hospital is still checking him over. Pete said he wouldn't know much more until they finished running some tests. All he really knows is that Jake swallowed a lot of smoke in the fire and that there are some burns."

"He's going to be all right, though, isn't he?"

"We think so. Pete couldn't get much out of them. You know how hospitals are. *'He's doing as well as can be expected and we'll know more when we get the test results.'* They won't say anything until they're good and ready—especially to mere business associates. Though from the way Pete talks about the crowds of frantic relatives swarming the hospital halls, even relatives aren't being told too much. We just have to keep waiting."

"I see."

Val's description of the situation only served to emphasize the point David had made earlier. No matter how much she cared, she had no legal rights to information about Jake's condition. She was dependent on the goodwill of his manager and the public news.

A new thought struck her, and guilt joined her other chaotic emotions. "What about the others? I was so shocked about Jake I never—"

"They're fine," Val set Nicole's mind at ease. "Most of them had gone Christmas shopping and weren't even at the hotel when it happened. George and Kevin were in the far wing away from the blast and were able to get out without any problem. In fact, they were the ones who confirmed that Jake had been at the hotel. He had invited them to have lunch with him downstairs just about a half hour before, but they'd already eaten." Having given what news she could, Val encouraged Nicole to be patient a little longer and said good-bye.

David returned to the living room when Nicole replaced the receiver.

"You heard?"

"Yeah." A grin of encouragement spread over his face. "Cheer up. Jake's too stubborn to let a little smoke slow him down."

"Maybe so, but he was unconscious." Nicole worried a loose thread on her robe, twisting it until it formed a knot. "And he was burned. Burns are serious."

"Good Lord, Nicole," David blustered. "He's alive. Smoke inhalation knocks people out, but he regained consciousness on his own. The burns are probably minor, too. If they were really bad the doctors would have mentioned it, even if they didn't give details. Relax. He'll be fine in no time at all."

Nicole finally let herself believe that the worst of the nightmare was over. She had to, the terrible fear that had gripped her since Val's first call had sapped all her strength and courage.

"Now . . ." David sat down and cupped Nicole's chin with his hand. "There's an old show business phrase that you might want to think about. It's kind of catchy. Can you think of what it might be?"

Nicole looked at him blankly. The world might not be as tilted as it had been moments before, but it had not yet returned to normal. She had no idea what he was talking about.

"This is Saturday," he hinted.

Still at a loss, Nicole questioned, "Yes?"

"The show must go on?" he prompted.

Comprehension dawned and Nicole straightened. "Oh, God . . . the performance."

"Right the first time, my friend. So I think we had better work out some kind of schedule that will take care of the finishing touches and still let us make up for some of the sleep we lost."

"But I can't leave. What if Val calls back?"

"I'm sure that organized little brain of yours will be able to work out a solution that will let you stay here until you have to dress. You can set up something if you have to leave before they call." David sat back. "I think you have one or two friends."

Arranging for people to take over the hectic preparations would give her something to keep her mind busy, if not solely occupied. She needed to act, to release the nervous energy that demanded that she not sit helplessly by worrying about Jake. Forcing the last of the cobwebs from her mind, she mused, "Maggie can supervise at the auditorium, and Mark's mother is taking care of the cast party. Lori's mother would probably help Maggie . . ."

"That's the spirit," David told her. "Why don't you sit down and make a list of what needs doing and people who might do them. I'll call Maggie so she can relate the news and assignments. After that I'll run down and buy us some breakfast rolls or something, and then we can both try to get a nap."

An hour later, Nicole curled up on her bed, still too keyed up to sleep. Her gaze fell on the dancing hippo propped in the corner of Brianna's bed. She remembered the night Jake brought it. He had been so teasing and lighthearted. So alive. The idea of him lying unconscious in the hospital squeezed her heart with fear.

Another face swam into her thoughts. Pale, and sharply boned, it was a face of fragile beauty and incredible sadness. Cathy. Starting with the summer when they were both fourteen-year-old apprentices with Adam's company, they had giggled, worked, and dreamed together. When David and Cathy fell in love, Nicole had envied her friend.

Always weight conscious, they both ate sparingly, but as time went by, Cathy ate less and less. She worked more and more. The pace she set for herself was frantic, and Nicole, seeing only her friend's dedication, didn't recognize the danger signals. Then, one June afternoon when they were eighteen, Cathy had collapsed in class. The punishment of driving exercise with no food to fuel it had taken its toll.

In the hospital, Cathy confessed her one regret to Nicole. "You know the only thing I'm really sorry about?" her friend told her softly. "I wish I had experienced love."

"But you and David—"

She'd smiled. "I mean sex. David wanted to, and so did I, but I was afraid. Now it's too late."

Nicole had protested, but Cathy ignored her. "I feel cheated, Nicole. I'll never know what it feels like to make love with David, or to have his child." She closed her eyes tiredly. "Don't be cheated. When you meet someone you want to love, love him. Don't worry about what other people will think." She reached out and touched Nicole's hand where it rested on the edge of the bed. "I wish I had."

Nicole hadn't ignored Cathy's admonition, and when she met Jake two months later, she'd followed her heart and not convention.

Four wooden stepladders stood on the auditorium stage, their mundane usefulness at odds with the elegant fittings of the ballet backdrops. Nicole mechanically directed the warm-up exercises using the ladder rungs as portable practice barres. Forced to leave her apartment at four o'clock to warm up for her own performance as the Sugar Plum Fairy, she'd left Maggie to hold vigil by the telephone in her apartment. She moved in a tightly controlled automation of discipline. Her mouth formed the words that led the dancers' movements, but her thoughts followed their own cadence.

"And *plié,* two ... three ... four...." *Hurry and call ... hurry and call ... hurry and call.* "And up, two ... three ... four. *Left tande.*"

She dismissed them at five-thirty to get into their costumes and to put on their makeup. Two workmen removed the ladders and began sweeping the floor free of miscellaneous bits of paper and dusty debris that might cause a dancer to slip. Referring to her ever-present clipboard, Nicole threaded her way through the network of cables taped to the floor of the wings to check if a problem in the snow scene lighting had been corrected.

"Nicole!"

She spun in the direction of Maggie's voice and rushed down the side stairs to meet her at the back of the auditorium.

"Val called. Jake's going to be fine." The elderly woman moved with surprising agility as she hurried down the aisle.

Nicole's heart lifted joyfully, and she hugged Maggie in delight. She scooped Brianna into her arms and swung her around in circles as she laughed in relief. They were both breathless when Nicole finally lowered Brianna back to the floor and turned to bombard Maggie for details.

"When is he coming home? Will he finish the tour, first? Is he still in the hospital?"

Maggie laughed, "Calm down, child. First, he's still in the hospital. He got burned when a piece of beam landed on him, but it's not too serious. The doctors want to keep him for a few days as a precaution. Second, he won't be finishing the tour because the smoke affected his voice—"

Nicole's face paled, but Maggie hurried on to explain, "Just temporarily. He'll be fine in a few days. They just don't want him to strain anything. He should be able to do his New Year's Eve concert in Los Angeles. And finally, he should be out of the hospital and home by Thursday or Friday." Maggie grinned, obviously happy to be the bearer of good news.

Nicole breathed freely for the first time since the early morning phone call that had sent her world tumbling around her.

"That's not all," Maggie added with a note of smug importance. "It looks like Brianna's daddy is a hero."

"What?"

"The reason Jake ended up in the hospital wasn't because of the blast itself," Maggie told her. "He was sitting at the far side of the restaurant when it happened. It seems he tried to help several of the people who were injured. He kept going back to be sure everybody got out. Apparently, he made one trip too many and passed out."

Nicole's brilliant grin of excitement died as she realized what might have happened. What she had feared had happened. Anger mixed with pride, confusing and tangling her reactions. He was safe, yet he had risked his life again and again by returning to the flaming building. Why couldn't he have waited for the firemen to do it? That was their job. He had a daughter to think of, dammit! One he had promised to return to!

Angry as she was, she knew he couldn't have acted in any other way. He wouldn't have been Jake otherwise. His natural reaction would be to do anything he could and not wait to see if others would do it. He had never been a selfish man.

"Val said to be sure to watch *Entertainment News* on Thursday night," Maggie continued. "They asked for a short interview with Jake after he arrives in New York. He should be able to talk a little better by then." Maggie chuckled. "All Jake can manage now is a raspy whisper, and Val said his voice reminds her of an obscene phone call she once got."

The description made Nicole laugh. The analogy was only mildly amusing at best, but she found that she couldn't stop laughing. Maggie caught the infectious release, and soon both women howled with relieved laughter as they stood in the empty theater aisle. Nicole's sides ached and she had to wipe away the tears when she finally pulled herself together.

"I've got to let David and the others know." Nicole managed to gasp through a new, if more controlled, fit of giggles.

The strained pall of uncertainty lifted from the entire cast and gave the Saturday performance an exuberance that surpassed opening night. During the snow scene, Nicole's snowflakes moved with precision, their white chiffon dresses sparkling with silvery elegance. Despite his lack of sleep, David put on a spectacular exhibition for the Russian dance. His leaps during the variations showed brilliance, and each movement flowed with crisp grace.

As the Sugar Plum Fairy, Nicole executed the intricate steps through a haze of euphoric joy, and the resulting performance created a magic of light and beauty. The euphoria extended through the well-wishers who swarmed backstage after the final curtain. Former students, parents, and a long line of supporters took pictures and congratulated the dancers. When many of them approached Nicole to express their enjoyment of the ballet, she responded with a broad grin and appropriate comments, but her thoughts and heart were far away in a London hospital.

Nicole was signing a tiny pre-ballet student's program when David tapped her on the shoulder.

"I'll take care of closing up the theater for you tonight. You go on over to the studio. Mark's mother set everything out for the cast party before she came to the theater, so all you have to do is make a polite appearance for half an hour, then you can go upstairs and get some sleep."

Nicole smiled gratefully but told him, "I don't think I could get to sleep yet, tired as I am. I'm too keyed up. Besides, you're as tired as I am."

"Hogwash! You're dead on your feet, girl. You haven't let yourself stop long enough to know it," Maggie scolded as she joined them. "You go home, smile graciously as you explain that you haven't had any sleep in thirty-six hours, then take a shower, two aspirins, and let nature take its course."

"Unlike you," David added, "I got a nap this afternoon while you were organizing the troops."

The exhaustion Nicole had ignored all day seemed to swell as she stood on the crowded stage, and she realized she should take their advice. "Okay," she gave in. "Just let me get out of my costume and makeup and I'll go to bed like a good little girl."

Once back at the studio, Nicole found it a little more difficult to bow out of the cast party than Maggie envisioned. Most of the parents knew about the drama that had cloaked the second ballet performance and several of them stopped her as she worked her way toward the back stairs. She had been trapped by a particularly long-winded parent who wanted her to know how carefully she had monitored the newscasts during the day when the phone in the lobby rang.

"Excuse me, Mrs. Thompson," she pardoned herself as she seized the opportunity to break away. "That might be David with a problem at the theater."

Mark's mother already had reached the lobby and lifted the receiver by the time Nicole arrived at the reception desk.

"I'm sorry I can't hear you. What?" Her eyes opened wide in surprise. "She's right here, I'll put her on."

Punching the hold button, she put the receiver on the counter. "You might want to take this call upstairs." She gave Nicole a conspiratorial wink. "It's Mr. Cameron."

Nicole turned and dashed for the stairwell, ignoring the startled looks her guests gave her as she disappeared. Fear made her hands shake as she lifted the receiver in her living room and pushed the button to release the hold.

"Jake, are you all right?"

Eleven

"I'm fine."

Nicole could barely hear the raspy voice on the other end of the line.

"I just called to see how the performances went."

"How th—! You might have been killed and you're calling me about a ballet?"

"Not just any ballet." The thin voice chuckled. The chuckle caught and became a cough. Several seconds passed before he could speak again. "I want to know how things went. You worked so hard—" Another cough stopped him from saying more.

"Jake, you shouldn't be talking. The smoke. You might damage your voice."

"My voice be damned," he wheezed. "Tell me about the show."

Nicole gave up. He would keep talking and strain his voice if she didn't take over the conversation and answer him. Mindful of the overseas rates, she related their success. "We cleared our costs and even made enough profit to put on a small spring recital," she finished.

Jake's occasional coughs had finally stopped while she talked, and she felt safe to ask him, "Why did you take such a chance, Jake?"

"I didn't think about taking chances. People were screaming and crying, I had to try to help." She could hear his labored breathing, then he went on, "I wasn't the only one, you know. There was a high-society dowager type at the next table who worked right along side me. Lady Ashford-Howell. She's the one who pulled the section of beam off me and dragged me out after I collapsed."

Nicole resolved to send a heartfelt letter to thank that unknown lady at the first opportunity.

"How bad are the burns?" she probed. "Are you in a lot of pain?"

"No, I was pretty doped up yesterday, but they're really not all that bad."

The choking cough took over again, and Nicole knew she shouldn't tax him anymore. "Jake, don't talk anymore. We'll talk when you get back."

"No, wait, Nicki," Jake protested through the raw hacking that grated through the line. "I want you and Bri to be at my place when I get home. I don't want to wait longer than necessary to see either of you. I'd ask you to meet my plane, but it'll be crawling with reporters." He paused for a breath, the appeal in his painful voice irresistible. "Val will give you a spare key. Say you'll be there."

"Yes. We'll be there."

She heard his sigh of relief catch in another coughing spasm at the same time as she heard a commotion in the background. An indignant protest preceded a new, firmly female and British accent on the line.

"I'm sorry, Mr. Cameron is not supposed to be talking to anyone for several days. He can call you again when his doctor has given him permission. Thank you and good-bye." Then the line went dead as the woman hung up.

A smile pulled at Nicole's lips as she realized that Jake had been caught by a very in-command nurse. Chuckling, she wondered how he had managed to make the telephone call in the first place.

Despite the rawness of his voice, he sounded strong and safe. Nicole knew now that she could truly believe in his return. After the matinee tomorrow the studio closed for the holidays. Classes wouldn't begin again until after the New Year. Once the props and sets were stored for the year, she could lock everything up and go to Beverly Hills.

When he returned, Nicole intended to see for herself that the burns were minor. She wondered if he would mind if she kissed them better . . . in a way quite unlike the healing kisses she bestowed on Bri. Thinking of Jake's demand that she wait for him to come home, and the fact that they had yet to settle where they stood with each other, she rather thought he might.

A huge yawn interrupted her thoughts. The party was still going downstairs. She could hear the opening strains of the party scene music, so she knew that Maggie had started the video tape of opening night's performance. She would watch it after she got to Jake's house. Right now, she was well overdue for sleep.

Picking up the receiver again, she dialed the lobby. This time Maggie answered.

"Hi, Maggie. I'm upstairs, and I'm going to go to bed. Would you send Brianna up?"

"Not until you tell me how Jake is. Mark's mother told me he called."

"Yes, he did." Nicole knew her voice reflected the joy that danced in her soul. "He still sounds raspy, but he'll be home a full week before Christmas. I'm going to meet him at his house when he gets back."

"Doesn't surprise me," Maggie returned. "Now I'll send Bri up, and you can tell me more in the morning. Good night, dear. I'm sure it will be a better one than the last."

"It couldn't help but be," Nicole agreed.

"That was very naughty, Mr. Cameron," Sister Georgina scolded as she firmly directed Jake back to his bed from the pay phone in the hallway. "We wouldn't want you to damage your voice permanently. After all, you promised me a ticket to your next concert in

England next year." She deftly arranged his sheets and smoothed his pillow as he settled back into the bed.

Jake eyed his nurse with disgruntled irritation. The tall, beanpole of a woman had run his schedule with skilled efficiency since he'd regained consciousness. "I'd just finished—"

"Don't talk, Mr. Cameron." She handed him a tablet and a pen. "If you must express yourself, do it in writing." She smiled and surprised him with a wink. "I'd be glad to post a letter for you if you'd like."

After she'd gone, Jake had to smile. He didn't begrudge his nurse her sense of discipline and obedience to doctor's orders—especially since he'd managed to talk to Nicole before being caught. Better yet, Nicole had agreed to meet him at the house.

Now that the doctors had canceled his tour he was more impatient than ever to get home. He wanted to hold Nicole in his arms again. He wanted to hear Brianna speak again. He wanted—dammit, he wanted to be a family.

A family. He thought about Nicole's parents and the distant way they showed their affection for their only child and grandchild. He wanted Bri to know the warmth of a close family, one like the one he'd grown up in. He needed to have Pete make arrangements for his parents to fly out for Christmas and meet their granddaughter.

He wondered if Nicole ever thought about having more children. He hoped so. He would love to be part of the times he missed . . . of watching Nicole's belly swell with his child, of watching his child come into the world, of watching Brianna playing with her brother or sister in the park.

He frowned. After the trauma she'd endured when Brianna had meningitis, Nicole might not want another child. Would she be afraid to take the chance of having something equally devastating happen?

Get a grip. You haven't even gotten the woman to agree to marry you, stupid. Take one thing at a time. If Nicole doesn't want any more kids, so be it. You have Brianna. That's enough. He pictured his daughter, with her pixie grin and her mischievous eyes. Bri was more than enough. She was perfect.

A melody floated to the surface of his consciousness, and he realized it had been present under the surface for several days before the fire. Words and ideas formed to match. He looked down at the tablet Sister Georgina had given him. There was no point in writing a letter. He'd be home before it got there. But he could bring them something. Maybe he could even convince Nicole that he meant what he'd said the morning he left.

Nicole pulled into the driveway and activated the remote release for the gate that protected Jake's home from overzealous fans. The neighborhood was quiet, tree-lined and unobtrusively well-to-do. The walls that separated many of the houses were of brick rather than concrete block or wood, and the glimpses she'd caught through wrought iron gates showed most of the homes to be set back from the street with broad, well manicured lawns.

As soon as she unlocked the door a few minutes later, she hurried to the hidden panel in the living room that Val had described when she delivered the keys at the Sunday matinee performance. The alarm switch disabled, she turned around to look at Jake's home.

Even though Jake had lived there for three years, it had the too-new air of a model home. She knew he traveled a lot, but she hadn't realized how much until now. The room was formal and beautifully decorated in a cross between country manor and men's hunting club. Deep greens with rich woods were warmed by rust and cream accents. The furniture was sturdy and at the same time graceful. It fit Jake's personality but held little of his presence.

Brianna had disappeared down the long narrow hall that ran the length of the house, and Nicole searched for her, gathering impressions of Jake's home as she looked in each room. They all seemed to reveal the same impact of having been selected by Jake's hand but rarely enjoyed by him.

Nicole found Bri in the den at the back of the house. Nicole stopped in the doorway. This was where Jake spent what time at home he had. A whisper of his aftershave clung to the walls and little traces of his occupation were strewn around the room. Though it was nothing like the modest apartment she'd shared with Jake so long ago, she felt like she belonged in this room.

A tidy stack of miscellaneous papers had been left on the edge of the wet bar. Several marked-up music scores had been left on the coffee table, and an old pair of running shoes had been kicked into the corner beside the door leading to the backyard. The less-than-company-perfection made her feel closer to Jake, and she walked to the recliner and ran her fingers over the headrest. The supple leather seemed to retain Jake's warmth.

The opposite wall held an entertainment center and a stereo system so elaborate that Nicole wondered if she dared attempt to operate it. Cautiously, she pushed the power button and was surprised to discover the radio tuned to a classical station. She'd always thought he listened to the station to humor her rather than for his own enjoyment.

Bri stood at the back door, trying to work the lock. Nicole looked out the sliding door to the backyard and saw a swimming pool covered with a black solar tarp. "No, sweetie, you can't go out there," she signed. "It's too cold to go swimming, and you must never go out to the pool without Daddy or me with you. Let's get your things out of the car and pick a room for you to stay in."

Val had told her that the house had four bedrooms with adjoining baths. Jake's room should be on the other side of the wall from the room where she stood. She resolutely turned to go out to her car and bring in her and Brianna's things. She would settle Bri and get out some of her toys before exploring which other rooms held Jake's essence.

Nicole crossed her fingers and pushed the plug into the wall socket. As she did, Brianna gave a delighted squeal and clapped her hands letting Nicole know that the lights hidden in the tiny Christmas village worked.

"Yes, they're very pretty," she agreed as Bri signed, her tiny fingers flying with excitement.

The village had been a present from Jake their first, and only, Christmas together. She wondered if he would recognize it. She adjusted the fluffy cotton base so the wires didn't show, then turned to survey the rest of her handiwork.

She'd set the Christmas tree up in the den since she felt closer to Jake there, but she wanted the living room to feel more homey. She'd banished the sterile smell with simmering pots of spruce and cinnamon scent, and in each of the deeply recessed bay windows on each side of the fireplace, she had arranged tableaus. On the left, angelic faced children in gold choir robes stood in a semicircle, their mouths held forever open in song. On the right, shepherds knelt before the Christ child in a traditional nativity scene. Poinsettia plants adorned the tables at each end of the couch, and bowls of nuts and brightly colored ribbon candies sat temptingly on the coffee table.

From where she stood beside the hearth, Nicole could see the sprig of mistletoe she had attached to the entry hall light with a bright red ribbon, and she smiled. She certainly wouldn't need the traditional plant to give her an excuse to kiss Jake. Still, knowing how many times she had crossed under the hanging crystal lamp in the two days since she and Bri had arrived it didn't hurt to have insurance . . . or incentive.

In the dining room, she'd strung artificial holly garlands over the window cornices and woven them into the chandelier above the oval oak table. A centerpiece of pine and holly encircled a six-inch round red candle which sat in the middle, waiting to be lit. This afternoon she intended to go shopping for a stocking to hang on the mantel beside hers and Brianna's on Christmas Eve. Nicole hoped Jake would be pleased with her efforts.

Fearing she'd lost Jake forever had made her realize she was foolish to hold out for a spontaneous declaration of love. His response to her taunt the morning he left had been automatic. But whether or not he really meant it, Nicole knew she could not let pride keep her from grabbing the happiness she wanted . . . even if it didn't last as long as she wanted.

If there was any way she could make him love her, really love her, she was determined to find it. With time, Jake might even come to love her as much as he already loved Bri. Much as the idea of a marriage like her parents' hurt, the pain of being separated from him would be greater. She couldn't bear years of having him touch her life as Bri's father, but never touching her.

For the time being, he wanted her.

When the day came that he no longer wanted her, she would cut her losses and live with the memories. She'd done it once, she would do it again. She wasn't sure how she'd survive a second time without Jake, but she'd deal with that if and when she had to. For now, she wanted their Christmas to be a family affair.

A tug on her sleeve brought her out of her thoughts and Nicole looked down to see Brianna holding out her purse. Her sober mood lightened and she grinned at her pint-sized helper. She had told Bri they would buy Daddy a stocking, for the fireplace when they finished setting up the Christmas village, and Brianna obviously meant to waste no time.

"Thank you, sweetheart. Let's get our jackets and then we can go."

She helped Bri into a cherry red parka, its white furry hood framing Bri's dark curls and blue eyes. She secured the zipper, slipped on her own coat, and led Brianna to the car. She didn't notice the dark blue sedan that pulled away from the curb as she left the driveway.

Nicole hurried through the crowds in the large enclosed shopping mall, her excitement growing as she absorbed the festive atmosphere. Christmas carols fed the tide of holiday shoppers with goodwill and a sense of how little time they had left to shop. Nicole wanted to find something to start the new year in the right direction. Hunting for a special gift for Jake filled her with hopeful challenge.

She passed the usual stores. Jake certainly didn't need ties or shirts or stereo equipment. Whatever she bought needed to be unique. Yet each store she entered seemed to offer variations on a tired theme, or worse, fad gifts of little value and less good taste.

She had almost given up hope when she saw the display in the toy store at the end of the mall. She grinned as she caught sight of the stuffed animals arranged to represent the characters of the old fairy tale, *The Bremen Town Musicians*. She remembered how the traditional fairy tale described the raucous noise made by the serenading farm animals and how they frightened away the thieves who'd gathered in an abandoned farmhouse.

In the toy store display, a donkey, dressed in sequined western wear, cowboy boots, and a Stetson hat, stood before a microphone. An electric guitar hung around his neck, and his mouth opened in a permanent song. The rooster, the dog, and the pig accompanied him on keyboard, bass, and drums. At their feet were displays of fairy tale books and children's songbooks.

Thinking of the hippopotamus, she knew she had found the perfect gift for Jake. Nicole led Brianna closer, then pointed the lead singer out to her. Brianna clapped her hands and laughed when Nicole suggested getting Daddy a toy like the one he had given Brianna.

Nicole stood at the counter writing the check when she first noticed the short, young man who attempted to catch Brianna's attention. He had taken a baby doll down from the shelf and was holding it out toward Bri and speaking to her. Brianna stared at him, her eyes large, their expression unsure. Excusing herself from the clerk, Nicole approached the man with a smile that was at the same time polite and wary.

"She doesn't understand what you're saying," she told him quietly. "She's deaf. What did you want?"

The man gave her a disarming smile, his expression lighting with understanding and something Nicole couldn't quite define. Whatever it was, it made her uneasy.

"I was thinking about buying this for my daughter. She's just about your little girl's age, so I asked if she liked the doll. I didn't mean to alarm you." He shrugged his shoulder as though embarrassed at the thought.

Nicole felt the tension leave her at the simple explanation. "Brianna already has a doll just like that, and she plays with it often," Nicole said. "I'm sure your little girl will enjoy it."

She turned to Brianna and held out her hand. Brianna took it, while she used her free hand to ask her mother who he was. Nicole explained that he wanted to buy something for his little girl. As they left the store, Nicole wished him a Merry Christmas.

Once back at the house, Nicole fixed Brianna and herself an early dinner. After they ate, Nicole helped Brianna wrap Jake's presents. When Bri was safely asleep, she brought out those presents for Brianna that still needed to be wrapped. She covered them in Santa Claus paper, before hiding them in the back of Jake's walk-in closet.

She cleaned up the paper cuttings and bits of ribbon, then picked up the last remaining shopping bag. After leaving the toy store, Nicole had given in to impulse and bought herself a new nightgown. She'd rationalized that her flannel gowns needed replacing.

As she pulled the black satin and lace gown from the bag, she admitted that she'd bought it to wear for Jake. The shop had sold several nightshirts of a more practical nature had she just wanted a new nightgown. She had even fooled herself that she gave them serious consideration before drifting over to the section of the shop where romantic satin, chiffon, and see-through lace drifted from the hangers.

She ran her hand across the smooth material, and couldn't resist slipping it on. The cloth whispered down her body, clinging softly to her curves and making her feel deliciously feminine. The fabric warmed to her body temperature as soon as it made contact, and its caressing softness made Jake seem closer. She knew she wouldn't change into flannel gowns again.

It was early, but she decided she might as well watch television in bed as in the den. She turned back the spread of Jake's bed, smoothing her hands across the satin sheets. She'd always wondered what they would feel like, and her first night in Jake's home she'd finally had her answer. Wonderful. Smooth, luxurious, and sensual, she couldn't have helped but be drawn to a nightgown of the same rich texture.

She slid between the sheets and pulled the comforter up to cover her bare shoulders. When she did, she closed her eyes and inhaled the subtle aroma of musk and cedar that floated up when the blankets were moved. Underneath the manufactured fragrances she detected the subtler, more comforting essence of Jake.

She'd known Jake's room and bed with the same instinct that had told her he used his den more than any other room besides this one. It was obviously larger and laid out to be the master suite, but Nicole knew that wasn't why she'd known it was the one he used. Nor was it the fact that his clothes hung in the large walk-in closet. It felt like Jake. Just like the den felt like him.

She reached for the remote just as the telephone rang.

"Nicki?" The voice at the other end had lost its rawness and Jake's normal resonant timbre thrilled Nicole with its vibrancy. "We landed in New York three hours ago, but it took us until now to get to the hotel. How are you and Bri?"

"Never mind us," Nicole brushed the courtesy aside. "How do you feel?"

"The only thing wrong with me is that I'm in New York instead of L.A. with you," he declared. "Something I intend to rectify tomorrow."

"Then it's a good thing Bri and I wrapped your Christmas present this afternoon."

"Oh, yeah? What'd you get me?"

Nicole laughed. "You'll find out Christmas morning."

She lay back against the pillows feeling the tension seep out of her body at the normal resonance of his voice. "You know you don't sound like an obscene caller anymore. Your voice must be getting better."

"Are you disappointed?" Jake countered. "I could think of some very provocative things to say to you if you wanted." He lowered his voice and asked. "What were you doing before I called?"

"I'd just gotten into bed—" Nicole broke off when she realized she'd set herself up.

She heard his breath catch, then warmth curled up through her body when he asked, "My bed?"

"Yes."

"What are you wearing?" The raw texture that toughened his words held a different note than the smoke had caused.

Nicole didn't answer. She couldn't. The satin gown flowed against her skin with an intimacy that reminded her of Jake, and a wash of liquid heat rose like a summer tide across her flesh. She felt like a child caught with her hand in the cookie jar.

"Nicki? Tell me. What are you wearing?"

"Just an ordinary nightgown." Silently, she cursed the defensive note she couldn't control.

"Honey, you could be swathed in flannel from your chin to your toes and it wouldn't be ordinary," he told her gruffly. "You know what I picture, though?" The receiver seemed to warm against her palm when his voice came through it. "Something sleek, and black, and satin. All the lights are off except for a single candle beside the bed. The flickering light catches the shimmer of the satin and it highlights the tips of your breasts and the soft curve of your hips."

Jake's words sent a heavy surge of solid need flowing through Nicole's body. She had to work to keep her breathing even and unaffected. "I don't think this a very good idea, Jake."

Her eyes had closed while he spoke into the phone, his soft words stirring her imagination until she could almost feel his hands tracing the highlights he described.

"Maybe not," he said with a suggestive chuckle, "but, I've got a feeling I might as well share my fantasy with you since it's going to drive me crazy all night anyway."

"Is this something like misery loves company?"

"I'd rather call it safe sex."

Nicole laughed in spite of herself. "You're terrible, do you know that?"

"Actually, you always said I was terrific."

She groaned. Then neither of them said anything for several seconds, the warm silence as tangible as if they were in the same room together.

"Nicki?" Jake's voice caressed her ear softly, and Nicole shifted lower into the bed and tucked the extra pillow next to her. Even with fresh sheets, she could pick up the faint wood and spicy scent of his aftershave on the pillow.

"Nicki, are the room lights on?"

"Just the one by the bed."

"Turn it off."

She felt mesmerized by the low seductive words, and reached to do as he asked. "It's out."

"So's mine." She could hear the faint rustling in the background. "Now, let me tell you more about what I see when I think about you in my bed."

"Jake—" Nicole's throat closed on the choked protest. Her body already tingled with the awareness his earlier words had created. Lying in the darkened room with his voice forming a cocoon of sensual fantasy around her, she could almost feel him beside her.

"Shhhh . . ." He quieted her choked protest. "Your hair is down, all soft and feathered on the pillow and the candlelight makes it look almost auburn where the lights shine on it."

Jake's breath came through the line with a sigh of pleasure. "I love your hair. It shimmers and flows over your body like a waterfall . . . and when we make love, and you lean over me, it caresses my skin like warm silk."

His words acted like a strange drug on her senses, making her aware of every pulsing beat of her heart, of every nerve ending.

"And when you straighten up, with nothing but your hair as a curtain to shield your body from me, I want to slide my hands through it and touch the warmer silk of your skin."

Jake's voice caught, and Nicole held back the moan of desire that welled up at his whispered words.

"I want to kiss every inch of your skin, I want to taste your sweet-salt flavor, I want my tongue to discover the texture of your breasts, your belly, your thighs . . ."

Heat spread through Nicole's body like molten lava, pooling hot and wet at the image he painted. She curled around the pillow in an effort to break the spell that made her ache with emptiness and need.

"If you keep this up," she managed to whisper into the receiver, her voice pitched low and breathless in spite of her efforts to sound normal, "neither of us is going to get much sleep."

Jake didn't answer for a moment. She could hear his uneven breath as he worked to steady it. "I guess you're right," he said at last. "We'd better get our sleep now, because when I get home I don't want to talk about my fantasies. I want to make them reality." Then he laughed, his chuckle low and evocative of sinful delights. "Satin sheets will have to do until I take you shopping for that sleek black gown." He laughed again, making Nicole's pulse race with anticipation. "It'll last for years since you'll never have it on long enough to wear it out."

Nicole pushed her grocery cart into the shortest line at the checkout counters. Bri sat in the kiddie seat looking at the bright pages of the Christmas storybook Nicole had agreed to buy her. After Jake's call last night it had taken several hours for Nicole to fall asleep. The dreams had been erotic and realistic. She cursed Jake's suggestive voice and sexy imagination. She hoped he'd had as restless a night as she had.

The woman ahead of her moved forward and began to empty her cart, and Nicole moved up until she could scan the magazines while she waited her turn. Her heart seemed to stop and her body froze in horror when she saw the cover of *World View*.

JAKE CAMERON'S HIDDEN LOVECHILD—
SINGER ASHAMED OF HANDICAPPED DAUGHTER

Twelve

The gossip tabloid's front page featured a grainy closeup of Brianna as she brushed her hair back, revealing the earpiece of her hearing aid. Beside it was an old picture of Jake taken from some music award ceremony, his date's face removed and Nicole's substituted, the angle of her head slightly awkward where it hadn't been placed quite right.

She pulled a copy of the magazine from the rack, her hands shaking with shock. The picture of Bri had been taken with a telephoto lens, and Nicole instantly felt exposed and vulnerable. She looked around the store, suddenly wary of so mundane an activity as buying food.

She studied the picture again, noticing the small patch of red in the corner. She recognized the bag from the toy store, and the image of the young man who'd approached Brianna flashed across her memory. No wonder he'd made her uncomfortable. That look he'd given her when she told him Bri was deaf. . . . It was all he needed to write the sordid lies that made Brianna a pawn to sell newspapers.

On an intellectual basis she'd known it wouldn't be long before the media knew about her and Brianna. Emotionally, she hadn't realized how traumatic seeing the distortions of her life smeared across checkout stands and television screens would be.

Fury alternated with fear as she stood with her gaze locked on the sordid headline. As long as she stayed with Jake, the three of them would be public property no matter if she married him or not. She wouldn't let Brianna become somebody's freak show for profit. She couldn't let Bri become an object of voyeuristic pity.

When Jake had used just this scenario as an argument that day he'd met Bri, she'd brushed it aside as though it meant nothing. Now it was real, and it terrified her.

She fought down the panic that made her want to run from the store. Suddenly abandoning her cart would only bring attention to her, and she wanted only to get away from possible recognition as quickly as possible. She unloaded her cart as fast as she could, grateful that the clerk worked with efficient boredom.

When she drove up to Jake's gate, she scanned the street, fearful that the man from the mall might be there. Mercifully, the street seemed as quiet and peaceful as the day she'd arrived. Inside the house moments later, she hurried to gather her things.

She couldn't stay in Jake's house. She had to get away before Jake came home, before the reporters came with him. Once they discovered her name they would follow her to the studio and invade her life in a media circus of gossip.

Brianna would be trailed and harassed for no other reason than her father was famous. Some idiot was sure to build a sob story about the irony of a man whose life revolved around music having a child who could not hear.

She was pulling Brianna's Christmas presents from behind Jake's suits when the corner of a box knocked a dusty white shoebox from the shelf. Nicole tried to catch it, but the lid opened and a shower of snapshots scattered to the floor.

She started to brush them aside, to leave them on the floor in her haste to get away, when she saw her own image staring up at her. Her breath caught when she recognized the piece of a photograph. It was a part of the publicity photo taken when she landed her first solo with Adam's company. Her hands shook as she picked it up.

It had been viciously torn into quarters so that the closeup image of her face was totally destroyed. Bits of clear tape, now curled with age, clung to the edge as though an attempt had been made to salvage the photo.

She scanned the floor of the closet, identifying other prints, some whole, some torn, then taped together. Unnerved, she knelt down on her knees and began sorting through the collection. She lifted the publicity picture fragment, placing it back into the shoebox. When she did, a faint whiff of dusty vanilla floated with it. The picture below it made her eyes sting with the sudden rush of tears. It had been taken on New Year's Eve when she and Jake had attended a costume party dressed as Romeo and Juliet.

Her costume had been an authentic replica of a Renaissance gown borrowed from a friend involved in reenactment organizations. She'd even worn vanilla in place of perfume at her friend's direction. At the moment the photograph had been snapped, Jake had whispered in her ear. His suggestion had been highly erotic, and the camera had captured the intent of his words and her agreement. They had left moments later.

At their apartment, Jake had removed each layer of her costume, slowly, and with thorough enjoyment. They'd made love to the soundtrack of the movie, never noticing when the tape ended.

A ragged tear marred the edge, but it hadn't been destroyed. Even in a rage, Jake had been unable to sever all the evidence of their time together. She set the intact picture in a separate stack, sorting it and others from those which had been torn. Only the impersonal, publicity photos had been ripped. The pictures of them together, or ones that he had taken of her, had been untouched except for the beginning tear on the New Year's print.

Nicole stared at the proof of Jake's hatred and love. He hated her for what she'd done, yet he'd loved her too much to rid himself of the pictorial memories. He hadn't even thrown away the ones he'd ripped, but kept them. Nowhere in the house had she seen reminders of other women in his life. She hadn't snooped through his drawers, but she knew she didn't need to. If anyone had given him a photograph while they dated, he'd thrown it out when they'd parted. No woman had made Jake feel deeply enough for him to keep mementos of their time together. No woman except Nicole.

She couldn't leave him again. The panic that had driven her after seeing the tabloid headline had disappeared the instant she'd seen what running had done to Jake five years ago. Had she learned nothing during the hours of uncertainty following news of the fire?

In the years after she left him, she'd always known where he was, what he was doing. She'd followed his rise in popularity, vicariously taking part in every success. The same public curiosity she was ready to run from had been the source of her information.

Her mind made up, Nicole stood and quickly put all the undamaged prints but the one from the party into the shoebox and returned them to the shelf in the closet.

Jake opened the door of his New York hotel suite, and Pete walked in, handing him a folded newspaper.

"I saw this in the lobby. I thought you'd better see it before the television interview this afternoon." Jake stared at the headlines, his anger growing as he read the article bannered on the cover of *World View* magazine.

"Call Don."

"Hang on, Jake. You know it doesn't do any good to sue these guys."

"I said, call Don." Jake walked over to the table and dropped the paper onto its surface with disgust, then turned back to Pete. "Tell him to get over to the house and make sure Nicole doesn't have to deal with the rest of the creeps this trash is going to bring out of the woodwork."

Pete visibly relaxed. "Good idea."

Jake circled the room like a caged tiger. Damn! He didn't need this. Nicole didn't need this. She'd scoffed when he'd talked about the tabloids that first day and he'd let her. To be honest, he'd used it as a scare tactic rather than a real threat.

He'd always had a good rapport with the press. He hadn't sought publicity, but he'd accepted the photographers and reporters with good grace and they'd responded in kind. His lifestyle hadn't been flamboyant enough to make him a target, only the object of public curiosity. His interviews had been frequent and candid enough to satisfy the public and give him reasonable privacy. So who had thought it necessary to lie in wait at his home, watching it . . . watching Nicole and Brianna?

He picked up the paper again and checked the byline. No name credit. It figured. The up-and-coming, hungry ones played the dirtiest. He'd bet his last dollar whoever took the pictures had made a giant step up the paparazzi ladder. His next picture and story would rate a byline.

He stopped pacing and looked at Pete. "I don't know why I didn't expect this. I should never have asked her to go to my place. Whoever took the pictures of them must have seen them there and put two and two together." He ran his hand through his hair in frustration. "And got five."

He walked over to the window and looked out at the New York skyline. A light snow fell, defusing his view and covering the grime of the winter streets.

He checked his watch. "Nicole knows we're taping the interview this afternoon and that it airs tonight, right?"

Pete straightened from where he'd settled on the couch. "Yeah." His furrowed brow almost brightened as he watched Jake's expression.

"Then let's get to the studio. I have an interview with people who will let me give them facts instead of suppositions and lies, and I certainly don't want to keep them waiting."

Nicole set her coffee cup on the end table, then switched on the television. The credits had just started and she took a sip, wondering how far into the program Jake's interview would be. She suspected it would be the latter part of the half-hour show, but she didn't want to take a chance of missing it.

Jake's lawyer, Don Bergoff, had telephoned to let her know he was coming, then dealt with the press who'd begun to show up within an hour of her return to the house. After talking to the reporters, he'd come in long enough for a cup of coffee and to reassure her that the men and women had agreed not to impose themselves on her any more than waiting outside the gates for Jake to arrive.

When the program's hostess introduced him, Jake smiled for the camera, and Nicole searched his face, noting the healing bruise on his forehead that showed even under the television makeup. She couldn't wait for him to get home so she could see for herself if his healthy coloring was real or the illusion of television lighting.

Though he sat in a relaxed pose, Nicole caught the sense of energy that reached through the camera to her and recognized the glint of anger in his eyes. It was clear that Jake knew about the *World View* story even if Don hadn't confirmed it.

Jake played down his actions in the hotel fire but focused on the overall situation and its effects on everyone involved. He praised the police and firemen for their organization and efficiency, the hospital for its care, and the public for their cooperation.

When asked about his change of appearance, Jake rubbed his freshly shaven jaw. His smile had all the menacing threat of his pirate image, reckless and dangerous. "I suppose the change is rather dramatic," he answered. "And it's one of the reasons for all the confusion during the fire. But I shaved my beard so my daughter could read my lips better."

Nicole clutched her coffee cup. *Here it comes.*

"You're referring to the little girl on the cover of this week's issue of *World View?*" The hostess held up the infamous tabloid.

"Despite the headline, yes." Jake leaned forward, looking directly into the television camera. "Brianna is only as handicapped as stereotyping and ignorance make her. I haven't hidden her, nor am I ashamed of her. She's the best thing that ever happened in my life, second only to meeting her mother."

Nicole gasped, and her startled jerk sloshed coffee onto her sweatshirt. Pleasure spilt over her whole body.

"The fact that I don't want Brianna exploited has nothing to do with her deafness and everything to do with the fact that she is only four years old."

"I take it you and her mother have no plans to marry?" The hostess asked the obvious question raised by the tabloid, and Nicole held her breath while Jake answered.

"I have plans." He grinned, and the determination in his expression warned Nicole that he was directing his words to her. "I'm still working on Nicole."

The pleasure grew, and Nicole suddenly realized she was smiling idiotically at the TV screen.

He turned his attention back to the hostess and gave her his most winning smile. "And if we can have a little privacy for a few more days, I ought to be able to change her mind."

The interview ended and the show went to a commercial. Nicole sat without moving. Her heart rate had jumped when Jake looked into the camera, and she'd had an instant image of candlelight and satin sheets.

Jake pulled through the gates and into the driveway, then shut off the engine. A lone cricket sent its greeting through the clear winter air. He studied the lights in the window to see if Nicole was watching for him. Don had met the plane and assured him she was safe and had been reasonably calm when he went to the house. But that had been hours earlier.

He'd stopped to talk to the reporters outside the grounds to win some cooperation. Now it was late.

In London, his last coherent thought before passing out in the clouds of smoke and flame had been that he would never see Nicki or Bri again. The thought had caused him more burning pain than the section of beam that had knocked him down. Now, after the publicity, he didn't know what to expect.

He wondered what Nicole's reaction would be when he told her they were getting married as soon as the publicity mess was out of the way . . . if he could wait that long. Before he'd left, she'd refused to consider it. But, then, she hadn't thought he loved her either. Did she still think he wanted Brianna more than he wanted her? He couldn't envision life without Nicole or Bri again. He wouldn't let it be a possibility.

SILENT SONG

If she still insisted that marriage wouldn't work, he'd use everything he could think of to change her mind . . . up to and including seduction. He smiled, thinking about their last night together, and his body tightened in anticipation. He rather liked that idea.

Of course it might be a little embarrassing for the minister to conduct a wedding for two people who looked like they'd just returned from their honeymoon suite rather than a couple getting ready to enter it. What was the old joke? Please, sir, you're only supposed to *kiss* the bride.

A slight breeze swirled a stray leaf across the driveway, and it brought the homey scent of woodsmoke.

Before he got carried away, he needed to think things through. If he walked in and announced his plans, he had a feeling she would be as stubborn as ever. She didn't like being told what to do. And all this hoopla probably had her spooked.

If he tried lovemaking, she'd claim it was proof that all they had was lust. And the last time he'd pushed too hard, she'd run rather than fight him.

Maybe he ought to act as though . . . as though what? As though he was far more patient than he was? As though he was willing to let Nicole set all the guidelines for their affair? As though an affair was enough for him this time, too?

He muttered an oath of frustration. Second guessing wouldn't get either of them anywhere. If he wanted to know what Nicole wanted, she had to tell him. If she didn't want what he wanted, then—he set his jaw— Then he'd damn well change her mind.

He got out of the car.

Nicole opened the door before Jake could use his key. Her long hair was unbound, and it clung, soft and silky, to the dark green flannel robe she wore. Hot need shook him when the lamplight from the hall made the rich tresses shimmer as warmly as the cinnamon that spiced the air.

The tense set of Nicole's shoulders and the wary, hunted look that shadowed her eyes kept him from pulling her into his arms and assuring himself she wasn't an illusion. She looked as though any sudden move would send her running to ground. He cursed the unscrupulous tabloid reporter who'd used Nicole and Brianna as stepping stones for his ambition.

He crossed the threshold, and the cinnamon mingled with the

sharp scent of freshly cut spruce, cloves, and nutmeg. A snap and a pop from the living room confirmed that the aroma of woodsmoke he'd noticed when he left the car came from his own fireplace.

"I wasn't sure you'd be here." His voice cracked, and he turned it into a cough to cover the emotions that tangled his insides at the thought of losing her again.

Nicole moved quickly, shutting the door and sliding her arm around his shoulders. "Come into the living room and sit down."

He let her fuss, feeling like a fraud for letting her. He hadn't coughed for days. Still, he enjoyed the quick fluster that changed the wary shadows in her eyes into green pools of concern for his well being. At least she didn't seem to blame him for making her a target for media hype. When he was seated in front of the glowing fire Nicole took a seat beside him.

"I told you I'd be here."

"That was before all hell broke loose." He reached out and touched a finger to the warm silk of her hair where it trailed down her shoulder. "Did you have any trouble with the reporters outside?"

"No. Don took care of them. I even sent some coffee out to them." She chuckled. "I figured a little goodwill couldn't hurt. Other than taking a few telephoto shots of the house, they've behaved pretty well."

"How's Bri? Did anyone bother her?"

"She doesn't have any idea there's anything wrong. Her greatest excitement was knowing you'd be here in the morning when she got up."

"Did it excite you to know I'd be here?" Last night's phone call had resurfaced in his imagination several times during the long night, and longer day, despite the confusion caused by the article in *World View*.

Nicole didn't look as distant as she had when he came in. He didn't want her to be distant. He wanted her to be close. He wanted to reel in the strand of hair between his fingers until she glided close to him, but the question in her eyes told him she knew how long he'd waited before coming in, and that fact made her wary.

Nicole plucked at the edge of her sleeves and avoided his eyes. "Yes."

Her confession sent his blood rushing and he couldn't stand the stiffness of their conversation any longer.

"Oh, hell!" He hauled her across his lap and kissed her with fierce possession. She didn't hesitate to respond, and Jake let himself sink into the pleasure of her mouth.

"I was going to be so civilized," he whispered raggedly as he lifted his mouth from hers at last. "But I've missed you more than I ever thought possible." He kissed her again, drinking in her sweetness like a man dying of thirst.

Nicole took his kisses with a greedy hunger. All of her fears faded with the solid warmth of his arms around her and his mouth on hers.

"I missed you, Jake. I was so scared."

"So was I," he admitted. He circled his hand around the back of her neck and pulled her back against his chest. "I was terrified you wouldn't be here when I got back."

Nicole heard the rapid beat of his heart where she rested her head. It matched the tempo of her pulse, and she slipped her arms around his waist, hugging him closer.

"I'd never do that to you again, Jake. Now I know what I put you through. All those hours of not knowing what had happened to you were unbearable."

She ran her fingers gently over the bruise on his forehead. It wasn't as bad as she'd feared, but it made her all the more aware of how close she'd come to losing him forever.

Jake leaned back and turned her face so she could see him. His gaze was hot and possessive. "The only thing I could think of when the beam fell was that I'd lost you again." He took a deep breath, letting it out slowly. "I love you, Nicki. I always have. I was just too wrapped up in my ambitions and plans all those years ago to realize it. And I was too angry and hurt to admit it after you left, but I loved you."

Nicole lay her finger against his lips. "I know." He licked its sensitive pad, and she almost lost her train of thought. "I found the box of pictures."

Jake stilled and his breath released a short cool current against her finger. His gaze locked onto hers, then shifted to the fire. Nicole knew she didn't have to explain which ones she meant.

"I was putting Bri's Christmas packages into the closet," she allowed herself that small alteration in the story, "and I knocked the shoebox by accident."

Jake kept his eyes averted, and his skin took on the ruddiness of masculine embarrassment. The fire popped and crackled in the silence as he stared into the flames. "Adam wouldn't tell me where you were— I went a little crazy."

Nicole heard the disgust in his tone and knew he hated that loss of composure. "You lost your temper, but you didn't lose control. You only ruined the ones that didn't matter."

"They all mattered."

"That's why you kept them?"

He met her gaze again. "And to remind myself that destruction accomplishes nothing. Tearing up the pictures didn't bring you back or make me any less guilty for driving you away."

"You've never been destructive, Jake. Look at all the beautiful music you've created."

"Did you know," he asked, "that every song on the first three albums is about you?" He reached up to stroke her hair, and Nicole felt the gentle persuasion of his large hands to the soles of her feet. "They're about betrayal and frustration and confusion and pain. But listen to the words in any one of them, Nicki, and none of them are about the loss of friendship. I never thought of you as my friend. You were my lover, but I never looked deeper to who you were."

He lifted her hair, smoothing it across his cheek before letting it slide back down to her shoulders. "I don't want to write any more pain songs. Life is too short to spend it hurting."

Nicole touched his hand. "That doesn't mean they weren't beautiful songs. They let people know they weren't alone and that life goes on. Don't forget about the boy who listened to your music when he was in the hospital. He needed those songs . . . even if it was his body that betrayed him instead of a person."

"Maybe so, but the point is, since I've been gone I've missed both my lover and my friend." He raised her hand to his lips, kissing her fingers. "Did you know that I like you? You are one hell of a woman."

Nicole looked up at him, a small smile curving her lips as she teased him. "Are you saying you'd rather be my friend than my lover?"

He turned her palm up and kissed it and the base of her thumb. "I want you to be both. If I can't make you believe that, how can I make you believe I love you?" He pressed a tender kiss against her forehead. "I do love you. Then, now, and always."

Nicole lifted her fingertips to trace his lips. "I believe you, Jake. I knew as soon as I found the pictures. If you hadn't loved me you would have thrown them away without a second thought."

Jake kissed her again, this time letting himself taste the sweet honey of her mouth. "You've never been out of my thoughts, Nicki. You never will be."

"Then come with me." Nicole sat up and took his hand. He stood with her and she guided him down the hall toward the bedroom. "I have something I want you to see."

Jake followed her, a smile forming as they neared their destination. "Do I show you mine after you show me yours?"

Nicole laughed. "It all depends on what you've got to show." She led him to the edge of the bed next to the table. When he sat down she picked up the ragged-edged photograph. "Here's mine."

Jake took the picture she held out. He recognized it immediately, his memory of that night etched in his mind almost as deeply as the night he'd nearly destroyed it in his pain. "That was some costume," he managed to say. "Who would have thought that many layers of clothing could be so sexy?"

He reached out to bring Nicole onto his lap. "Almost as sexy as the woman wearing them." He kissed her, loving the rightness of her soft body against his after the weeks apart. "Do you think you could borrow that dress again sometime? We could have a very private party . . . for two."

"I suppose." Nicole took the photograph from Jake and put it back on the bedside table. "But right now I have something else I'd like your opinion on."

"Oh? What's that?" Jake watched the teasing light in Nicole's eyes as she stood up again, and resisted the urge to pull her back into his arms. He found himself watching Nicole's hands with fascination as she toyed with the zipper of her robe. He'd been right. She was sexy as hell, even in flannel.

"Do you believe in ESP?"

Startled, he tore his gaze away from her hands and looked up. His body hummed with anticipation. "I don't know . . . why?"

"You see, last night I decided there must be something to it. After all, how else could you have described my new nightgown so accurately?"

Nicole let the zipper open and shifted her shoulders so the robe parted and fell to the floor. The black gown underneath made Jake's mouth go dry, and he swallowed reflexively.

"Black . . . satin . . . clinging. The only thing you didn't mention was the lace. But three out of four ain't bad."

She bent down to pick up the flannel robe, and the gown's low neckline gave him a glimpse of pale flesh. Desire gathered into a heavy pool of pulsating heat as Nicole teased him. "You—" Saliva had returned in force, and he felt like Pavlov's dog. "You had that on last night when I called?"

"Yep."

"You said it was an ordinary nightgown."

"I lied."

He swallowed hard. "You sure did."

She stepped closer, and he reached out to run his hands along the sleek satin covering her breasts. The satin changed shape as her body responded to his touch. His nerves sent out Morse codes of expectation, firing his own reactions.

He cupped the resilient fullness of her breasts, loving the way they filled his palm, then eased down as gravity tugged at their soft weight. Both tips pressed against the dark, shimmering fabric. His breath took an uneven path and his heart raced after it.

"I don't suppose you bought any candles at the store this morning?"

Nicole gestured to the pewter candle holder next to the lamp on the table. "Your fantasy is my command." She sounded like a fantasy. She whispered the teasing cliche as though it was tantalizing truth. Beside the candle holder were two small boxes. The second one held matches.

His hands shook slightly as he reached for the matches and lit the candle. As the heat melted the wax seal of the wick, the subtle scent of ripened vanilla lifted into the air. It filled him with images of unlacing heavy Renaissance velvet to reveal flesh as satiny smooth as the gown that covered her now.

He switched off the lamp and tried to remember to breathe as the candlelight cast Nicole in erotic highlight and shadow. He reached for the other box before pulling her down to the bed with him.

Thirteen

Nicole followed him willingly. He kissed her hot and hard, and her teasing banter melted with the heat of it. Now that he held her, she couldn't wait for teasing or gentle sharing. She wanted to take and be taken. She wanted the most basic proof that she had not lost him to fire and smoke.

She unbuttoned his shirt, pushing it from his shoulders with frantic haste. She needed to know that he was real, and whole. She needed to see for herself the marks on his body and assure herself that they would pain him no more than a short time.

Jake gave her no time to inspect his healing burns or bruises and he proved that he, too, needed to reaffirm life and vitality and each other. They came together quickly, barely taking the time to free Jake from his clothes or to take precautions. Nicole found release quickly and with savage intensity. Jake followed her lead, and they fell through time and pleasure together.

They lay together for several minutes, catching their breath and savoring the primitive satisfaction that acted as a catharsis for the traumatic weeks apart. Jake shifted her until she lay flat against the satin sheets. Then he draped his knee possessively across her thigh and his arms surrounded her with territorial affirmation. He nuzzled her neck and growled.

"Lady, I hope you got a lot of sleep last night."

She grinned wickedly. "Even if I didn't, I don't intend to sleep tonight."

Jake laughed.

The feline contentment that warmed Nicole was more than the result of physical satisfaction. Jake was home, and she felt whole again.

She'd watched him talk to the reporters before turning into the driveway and was impatient with their demands on his time even though she knew such demands were part of his life. When he'd sat in the car, his face turned toward the windows for nearly ten minutes more, it had been all she could do to stay inside and wait for him to come to her. She wanted to forget the world and live in his fantasy tonight.

She looked up at him, loving the predatory gleam in his blue eyes. The subtle scent of vanilla blended with the musky passion that still shimmered, waiting to flare again after they'd rested. After the long nights of inhaling Jake's essence in the big empty bed while she waited for him to return to her, she wanted to absorb him into her pores. Her fingertips mapped his broad chest, tested the tensile strength of his shoulders, and traced the late-night stubble of his jaw.

A cloud scent rose in the warmth of their embrace, bringing with it the pleasure of Jake's lips caressing her shoulder. He wore the clean woodsy aftershave that had encircled her dreams as she curled around the pillows of his bed the past few nights. It merged with the vanilla of long-ago reality, and she knew she would do everything in her power to make Jake love her as much as he wanted her. He nibbled the sensitive skin below her ear and Nicole felt her pulse respond to the gentle pressure of his lips.

She gave him a mild push then followed him as he rolled over until she lay half across his chest. The change in their positions delivered new tactile messages and fired off anticipatory flashes of heat deep inside her body.

She stroked his muscular shoulders and slid her fingers into his thick hair. The primitive need to claim and be claimed grew and she leaned down and boldly tasted his lips. He grunted with pleasure and kissed her back, probing and spreading the flavor of mint and male into her mouth and soul.

Nicole was the delicious reality in his fantasy, and Jake wanted to drown in her rich flavor. He drank from the textures of her tongue, her lips, the inner recesses that held a honied sweetness that made him dip into them again and again.

She moved above him, shifting his focus to the soft rounded breasts that rubbed against his chest. Nicole still wore the satin gown, and her breath caught, then quickened when he moved her until his mouth dampened the tender fullness it covered. He slipped the thin strap from her shoulder and exposed one perfect breast. He kneaded its softness until the tips of her nipples formed hard nubs that pulled tighter as his palms pressed against them.

He circled the dark flesh with his tongue. She leaned into him and she gave a ragged gasp that sent desire ricocheting through his body. He slid the other strap down and paid homage to her beauty again. This time he suckled, pulling the pebbled surface deep into his mouth. He teased the other with quick hard strokes of his hand. She cried his name, and his pulse leapt with triumphant anticipation.

She sat up beside him, her face flushed with passion and her eyes luminescent with pleasure. "My turn," she whispered.

Her hair fell in warm cascades across his body as she knelt over him, brushing his chest with hot, damp kisses that sent his senses reeling. Her slender fingers explored his flesh, her nails lightly making contact when she curled her hands, then spread them wide again as she traced the contour of his torso.

Her hands strayed lower, and Jake sucked in a sharp breath of pleasure as his pulse concentrated its throbbing heat to the sensitive area Nicole stroked and teased.

He heard her intake of breath when she felt his response, then she gave a low, seductive laugh. "Yes. Let me feel what I do to you." Her hands left his body briefly to shrug out of her gown, then their warmth returned, fitting him with protection and firing him with an aching need.

Her hair brushed over him again, and this time she moved to rub against him with catlike enjoyment. Her perfumed and rich woman scent floated in and out of his consciousness as she moved, driving him higher and higher with the feel of her as she grazed his flesh with hers. She kissed him again, and he wanted to feast on the banquet of flavors, textures, and moans that filled his mouth.

He'd dreamed of them like this. Dreamed, but never believed the time would come again when she would love him so freely, so wantonly. The night before he'd left for England had been an answer to the attraction they couldn't deny, but tonight promised a new beginning.

He rolled her back under him and took her with a hoarse cry of possession. She rose to meet him, and they began the rocking, sense-flooding rhythm of passion that sent them beyond the limits of awareness. When he felt her rhythmic pulses tighten around him, his pleasure built to a rush of heated release that held his body rigid with completion.

He sank down beside her, pulling her close until her cheek rested on his shoulder and her warm breath feathered against his neck. His hand rested in the sloping indentation of her waist, his fingers curving across the sleek smoothness of her belly. "I hope you bought a big supply of those things, honey," he whispered in her ear. "Because I don't want to go out to a drugstore in the middle of the night with a bunch of tabloid reporters dogging my tail."

He felt her mouth curve into a smile. "There are more in the drawer, Boy Scout."

Nicole adjusted the neckline of the cream-colored dress she wore. The satin bodice crisscrossed from her shoulders to her waist, forming a deep "V" neck that she held in place with a carefully located snap. A slender skirt of velvet wrapped around with a soft drape into a straight skirt. She viewed herself critically, knowing her image would soon be blazoned across more entertainment papers than the *World View*. Nervously, she licked her lips and smoothed the braided figure-eight coil that pulled her hair high on her head.

When the doctors declared Jake fully recovered from his smoke inhalation, she'd been relieved to have them confirm that Jake would suffer no lasting effects. But when she discovered that Jake saw his New Year's Eve concert as the perfect opportunity for the three of them to appear in public, she'd been ready to have the doctors give him another examination.

Jake insisted that the best way to deal with the tabloids was to give them picture taking opportunities while giving interviews with the more mainstream entertainment press. She held her hand over her stomach, hoping its nervous rolling would settle. She supposed he was right, but her intellect and her emotions didn't always agree.

A small face peeked around her in the mirror's reflection. Brianna circled her hand around her face, then pointed at Nicole.

"You look pretty, too," Nicole said.

She lifted Bri onto the vanity's chair so she could see herself full-length in the mirror. Brianna wore a floor length blue velvet dress that made her eyes blaze with color. The dress was trimmed in creamy ecru lace at the neck and sash. Her long dark curls were held back from her face by a matching blue velvet ribbon.

Nicole checked her watch. They needed to leave soon if they were going to get to the amphitheater in time. She fingered the unfamiliar weight of the square-cut diamond ring on her left finger. Jake had scheduled an interview with *People Magazine* to announce their engagement, and she was supposed to be there an hour early to be part of it.

She licked her lips again. If she had gone to the theater earlier with Jake she could have avoided some of the pandemonium her separate arrival would bring, but other than to avoid photographers, there'd been no reason for her to leave until now. She would have felt like a coward if she had taken the easy way out.

She still believed that she and Brianna would be nothing more than a ninety-day-wonder, especially after Jake and Nicole announced that they were getting married. She smiled wryly at her reflection. She just had to get through the ninety days.

The phone rang and Nicole saw that it was the line to the front gate. She pushed the button and picked up the receiver.

"Hi, Pete. Yes, we're ready." She dialed the code to release the gate, then helped Brianna down from the vanity chair. "Come on, sweetheart, it's time to go meet Daddy."

Pete drove them around to the artist's entrance where several reporters and photographers already waited for them. Nicole's stomach knotted, and she hoped she'd prepared Bri for the circus that awaited them. Brianna had her face pressed against the window and stared with wide, inquisitive eyes at the bright lights and milling crowd.

The car stopped and Nicole helped Bri out of her car seat. Then Pete opened their door and Nicole braced herself for the blinding flashes and waving microphones. Bri clung to her hand as Nicole smiled blindly and hurried after Pete through the corridors the security people had made for them.

"Smile!"

"Look this way!"

"Give us a wave!"

"Get a load of that ring!"

"Over here!"

"Now, over here!"

She made it through the doorway and the sudden silence that followed the slam of the soundproof door was a welcome relief. She stopped to be sure Brianna hadn't been frightened by the mad dash though the confusion of lights and waving reporters.

Brianna's eyes sparkled with excitement. She held up her index finger and waved it in the air.

"Daddy's right here," Jake said as he came into sight from the hallway.

Nicole pointed, and Bri laughed when Jake scooped her up into his arms.

"I should have known she'd enjoy all the attention," Nicole said. "I guess it didn't seem much different than all the well-wishers who come backstage after the ballets."

The interview didn't take long and went better than Nicole had hoped. When the writer asked about their wedding plans Jake gave Nicole a conspiratorial wink. "We'll announce it after the fact," he answered. "We'd rather not have helicopters circling overhead and drowning out our vows."

The interviewer laughed. After he turned off his tape recorder and the photographer got them to pose for a group picture, they left.

"Am I supposed to see you in this dress?" Jake teased her when they were alone again.

"Since I had to be here for the interview, I don't see how you could help it." She let him pull her into his arms and kiss her. "Maybe if you don't see my hat until the wedding, this won't bring us bad luck."

He kissed her again and chuckled. "I think the bad luck is supposed to happen if the groom sees the bride on the day of the wedding . . . and we're getting married after midnight, remember. We're still safe."

"And if we're going to avoid that tabu, then I'd better get to my seat."

The lights dimmed as Pete led Nicole and Brianna to their seats in the front row. Val, David, Maggie, Adam, and both his and her parents already occupied the rest of the row. She was grateful for the semi-darkness when she felt the speculating eyes of most of the audience on her and Brianna.

The curtains opened to reveal Kevin, Marty, and George on

stage. They played the lead-in music, then Jake strode across the stage to take his place at the microphone. Nicole could feel the audience shift its attention to the stage, and she was finally able to sit back and relax a little.

He opened with his first major hit, and the crowd clapped and cheered their approval. From there he swung into a more recent song, and the evening settled in to an entertaining and crowd-pleasing show.

Nicole barely heard the words as she drank in the sight of the man she loved doing what he did so well. His voice resounded with the warm, caressing throb of sensual masculinity that made her skin tingle with awareness. It was as though his voice stroked her as thoroughly as his hands had the night before.

The audience had no idea that the tux Jake and the rest of the crew wore weren't in honor of the New Year, but because of the minister sitting unnoticed by the crowd as a guest of the performance. Nor did they suspect that the flower and balloon decorated arch behind the music equipment would soon serve as a wedding chapel.

During the intermission, Nicole and the others went backstage and enjoyed a glass of champagne and a chance to talk.

"I'm not too sure I ought to condone this marriage."

Nicole turned in surprise when Adam spoke. Jake's arm tightened possessively around her, and his grin of triumph faded to an expression of surprised irritation.

"I didn't think you still had doubts," Jake said.

Adam gave a bark of laughter. "I'm not worried about the two of you," he said with another chuckle. "I mean I don't much like losing one of my best lead dancers to Nicole's studio."

David drifted over in time to catch the end of the conversation. "How come you never said that during salary negotiations, Adam?"

Jake grinned again when he realized Adam was referring to the partnership David and Nicole had agreed on in order to keep the studio running without her having to commute each day. David would take over the daily operations, and Nicole would help him with the two productions much the way he had helped her in the past.

"Look at it this way, Adam," Jake said. "You may be losing a dancer, but I'm gaining a wife. I think it's a fine idea."

"So do I," Nicole agreed.

The warning buzzer sounded and they returned to their seats for the second half of the show.

Nicole had watched the rehearsals almost every day since Jake had returned and knew the program by heart, so she was surprised when he handed his guitar to Kevin before the last song. The stage lights dimmed until a single spotlight held Jake in its bright beam. He cleared his throat, and the audience stilled to a complete silence.

"Ladies and gentlemen, I'd like to do a special song before I wrap this up. Most of you probably know that I've discovered a pretty special person who is going to be a part of my life from now on." He gave his rakish pirate grin. "That's not to say her mother isn't pretty special, too."

The audience laughed and Nicole felt her cheeks heat.

"Actually, her mother is more than pretty special." He looked in her direction, and Nicole knew he tried to see past the glare of the spotlight to where she sat. "But I wrote this song for them while I was in England, and I want to share it with them . . . and you."

Kevin stepped closer and began to play a series of chords as Jake moved the microphone out of the way. Jake began singing softly, and Nicole felt tears sting her eyes when his hands began moving with clear flowing purpose. The tender words left her in no doubt that the song was for her, even though he signed them for Brianna. By the time he sang the final words, *So come with me and sing our silent song of love,* Nicole knew she'd never loved him as much as she did at that moment.